Jingle

to the

Rescue

By Helen Haraldsen

Illustrated by Steve Hutton

Jingle Bella to the Rescue

Illustrated by Steve Hutton

Editing, Cover Design and Formatting by Let's Get Booked:
www.letsgetbooked.com

Paperback ISBN: 978-1-913953-11-9

eBook ISBN: 978-1-913953-12-6

Book 3

This book is dedicated to all the working dogs out there, providing valuable assistance to their owners and members of the public. From service and assistance dogs, police dogs, search and rescue, detection, herding, hunting, pulling sleds, guarding, therapy and companionship, dogs help us in so many ways.

A special mention to school reading dogs who are working with a number of charities who support child literacy by visiting schools to help children develop a passion for reading.

ONE

Bella the Dalmatian had only been living with the Daleys, Petra and Lucy for a couple of days, but she already loved it. The Daleys had bought her a bed of her own, but she mostly ignored it, preferring instead to snuggle up with Petra the Pointer or Lucy, another Dalmatian, in their beds. She already loved her new friends, whom Mr Daley had started calling her aunties: Auntie Meist and Auntie Leopard, and whenever she was awake, wanted to play with them. Sometimes, when she got too excited, she'd nip too hard with her still-sharp puppy teeth. Despite her pledge to be more patient, Petra couldn't help growling and getting grumpy when Bella's nips hurt her. But Lucy never, ever growled or snapped at the pup. If she wanted to bring playtime to an end, Lucy would simply pin Bella down and start licking her face. The young dog found this so blissful, she would stop being a 'Bella

Bomb' as Mr Daley had started to call her, and relax while Lucy mothered her. She often found it so comforting, she'd go to sleep.

"That's how you deal with naughty puppies," Lucy would say, reminding Petra that she'd also been a very naughty puppy but had received nothing but patience from Lucy when she'd arrived to join the family a few years ago.

A couple of days after Bella's arrival, the Daleys took the three dogs for a walk in the fields near their home. Petra was being kept on her new extendable lead as the Daleys were terrified of losing her since she'd gone missing twice in the space of a few months.

Petra strained against the lead. She was desperate to streak off across the fields into the nearby woods and run free, chasing the scents that would lead her back to the compound where dogs and their puppies remained trapped and helpless, but she could not. The lead held her in place. She rammed her neck against the collar, but it was no good. She couldn't escape.

Lucy and Bella walked beside her, hoping that their company would distract her, but Petra barely noticed them as she pulled.

Petra's first disappearance was an accident: she'd fallen through the rotten covering of a well while dashing about in the woods looking for deer to chase. The second time, Petra had gone off on a mission to rescue the local vet's dogs who'd been stolen and ended up in a puppy farm, but the Daleys didn't know that. They thought Petra had been stolen too. And since she was prone to disappearing whenever they let her off the lead, she wasn't being allowed off it. Lucy and Bella were, but they sympathetically stayed by Petra's side so as not to leave her out.

Bella's tail wagged the whole way as she enjoyed taking in the sights around her. Her previous owners never took her for walks before she came to live with the Daleys and her happiness was clear to see. Lucy and Petra had too much on their minds to enjoy the walk.

"When you arrived the other night, you said you had a plan about how we'd rescue the dogs still left at the puppy farm, since Petra can't get back to them. Did you mean it?" Lucy asked Bella as they walked side by side with Petra. "I've been watching the news and there have been no sightings of the thieves. If they haven't gone back to where the dogs and puppies are, they won't have had any food or water for two days. We have to act now and get them rescued."

"Yes, I think I have an idea that could work," Bella replied, still wagging.

"Well, spill the beans then," said Lucy, with uncharacteristic impatience. "We can't afford to wait for the humans to sort it out."

"Exactly," Bella said, looking at Petra. "Do you remember when the police found us in that hut we were sheltering in, after we escaped the thieves?"

Petra nodded, "yes...why?"

"Well, that's where I got my idea from. There weren't just human police officers..."

"There were police dogs too." An image of the German Shepherds wearing their 'police dog' harnesses popped into Petra's mind as she remembered waking up to find herself and the stolen dogs surrounded.

"Exactly," Bella said again. "We need to get the police dogs to lead the human police to the puppy farm."

Petra let out a big huff of disappointment. She knew she mustn't snap at the pup. She was only young and trying to help, but this plan could never work. Petra knew she shouldn't have got her hopes up based on the idea of a puppy, but she couldn't help it. She'd promised the boxer she'd go back and get them out but now she couldn't. The Daleys were acting like bodyguards and she never got a minute to herself anymore. She'd only need a couple of seconds to slip away and head back across the country to where the puppy farm lay hidden many miles away, but she was under constant surveillance.

"How would we let the police dogs know where they are, though?" Petra asked, as kindly as she could.

"And even if we could let them know where the place is, what then? How would the dogs get the humans to the right place?" Lucy pointed out. "It's a very good idea, but it's just not possible."

"I think it is," Bella replied, carrying her head as high as her tail, "and I'll prove it."

TWO

"We need to start now, before we get taken back home and indoors," Bella said. She ran ahead of the other dogs onto a raised grassy mound and lifted her head into the breeze. "Help, help, help," she barked.

"What's she doing?" the Daleys and Lucy asked at the same time.

"I'm seeing if there are any dogs in range who can pass a message on to the police dogs. Help, help, help!" she yapped again.

Petra and Lucy looked at each other helplessly as Mrs Daley called to Bella to get her to come back to them. The Daleys were concerned by their new dog's behaviour, as Bella stood like a spotty statue, staring into the distance. There was no reply. Just the sound of birds tweeting in the trees and the occasional whoosh of a car on a nearby road.

Since Bella was ignoring Mrs Daley, she stepped forward and attached a lead to Bella's collar. "Come on girl." She spoke gently to the young dog. "What are you barking at? There's no-one there."

She gave a gentle tug on the lead, but still Bella remained frozen in place.

"It's like she's waiting for something," Mr Daley said to his wife as she gave Bella another tug on the lead. Even though he didn't know it, Mr Daley often made accurate descriptions about what the dogs were up to. He didn't realise how clever they really were. Just as they turned to leave, an answering bark was carried to their ears. To the Daleys, it sounded like a faint yap in the distance, but the dogs heard much more. They heard the voice of a Jack Russell terrier ask, "Who's that? What do you need?"

"Puppies and dogs are being held in a prison and need rescuing," Bella barked back rapidly. "We need to get their location to some police dogs." Petra pulled on her long lead to stand beside Bella and she barked into the wind, "I'm Petra. I know the way. I can give directions."

"Petra?" the voice floated back to them. "Are you the dog from the news? Who pushed a boat full of dogs across a lake?"

"Yes, she is," Lucy woofed, her chest puffed with pride. Petra's heart skipped a beat. This dog - wherever it was – knew all about her!

By now the Daleys were frantically shushing the dogs and pulling them all away from the mound, wondering why all three had started barking at some dog miles and miles away. They'd never done this before.

Petra continued to bark, even as she was being pulled away. She listed landmarks near the puppy farm, and even some of the names she'd been able to read on footpath signs as she passed them. "Get this message to police dogs in the area. Tell them they must get their humans there urgently. Dogs are trapped with no food or water. They need help."

They didn't hear the Jack Russell's reply. They weren't certain if Petra's message had even been received, but there was nothing they could do as the Daleys were marching them back towards home, tutting about their strange behaviour.

"Whatever gave you the idea to do that?" Lucy asked later when the dogs were alone in the kitchen. "To just bark out into thin air and expect to get a reply? I've never heard of such a thing. It's just not what dogs do. We only bark when there's something to bark *at*."

Bella explained that in her previous home, she'd spent a lot of time on her own in the garden when her humans didn't want to be bothered with her. She'd heard dogs in the neighbourhood barking at each other, but it was usually things like, "Hey, you, this is my garden. Don't you even think about opening that gate and coming in here. I'll get you!" or, "Cat! Cat, come here cat!" or, "Yeah, you stay on that pavement. I'm watching you. Don't you come near my human. Stay over there!" But one day she heard something else.

"I didn't know the dogs in my area as I never got taken for walks, so I didn't know who it was, but I heard one dog bark out, 'Alfie? Where were you today? I missed you in the park.'

"Another dog barked back, 'Yeah, the humans got up later than usual this morning and were rushing about like idiots. I didn't get out for my walk. Hopefully things will be back to normal tomorrow and I'll see you there as usual.'

"Then the other dog said something like, 'good, cos I've got a new ball I want to show you. It squeaks!'

"It was the first time I'd heard two dogs have an actual conversation, not just warn dogs or people away from their gardens or humans. I didn't give it much thought, but then I realised it could be a way for us to pass the message about the puppies on to dogs who could help."

Lucy looked at the young Dalmatian with admiration. Lucy considered herself pretty wise and knew that Petra always looked to her to do the thinking when it was needed, but she'd underestimated the pup. Bella may only be young, but she wasn't daft. Like Lucy, she was also a thinker and a problem solver. Petra had told her how it had been Bella's idea to use the skateboard to assist Gomez and Gizmo in their escape from the puppy farm as neither of them could walk very far, which also gave the wayward husky a job to do and stopped her from wandering off. In future, she wouldn't be so quick to dismiss Bella's ideas and would listen to her more carefully.

***

That night, when the dogs were all squashed on the sofa on top of the Daleys, Lucy waited anxiously for the news. Since learning about the theft of the vet's dogs, and of Petra's rescue mission from the TV news the Daleys liked to watch in the evening, Lucy watched every night now too. She was waiting to hear if there was anything about the puppy farm and the thieves. Also desperate for news of the dogs she'd had to leave behind, Petra looked right at the screen too, rather than snuggling in for a nap as usual. Only Bella, who didn't know what the TV was, went to sleep.

There were pieces about the local secondary school, a proposal for a new supermarket, a human who was doing a sponsored cycle around the country for charity and something about a man who'd been to court and sentenced for dangerous driving, whatever that meant, but there was nothing about the dog thieves or a police raid on a puppy farm.

"I wonder if Bella's plan worked?" Lucy said when the news ended and another programme came on. "Maybe it's not enough. Will other dogs work hard enough to pass the message on and make sure it reaches the police dogs in the right area? Will the police dogs be able to do anything? Even if they try to tell their human officers about it, humans rarely know what we're saying to them, even though *we* usually understand *them*. They're not very clever, are they? Maybe the dogs won't be able to make them understand."

Petra was also anxious and had been hoping to see that the trapped dogs had been found. "We'd better try to do some more barking in the morning," she said, "and see what we can find. Time is running out."

When the Daleys went to bed that night and left the dogs in the kitchen, only Bella slept. Lucy and Petra lay awake in the darkness, worrying and fretting over the dogs in the puppy farm. Were they still there? Had the thieves gone back to look after them, or abandoned them to save themselves? Not knowing was unbearable and the comfort of sleep, impossible. The two knew they could not rest until the dogs and puppies were safe.

THREE

The next morning's walk took them across fields to a nearby river. It was getting too cold for swimming as it was early October, and Petra was still on the lead, so they stuck to the path. None of them were in the mood for paddling or swimming for sticks, anyway. There were far more important matters to deal with. Play time would have to wait.

"You two are going to have to run off into those woods and do some more barking," Petra said as they walked along. "I can't come, but you two are off the lead. You can get away for a few minutes."

"But we're miles away from any houses here," Lucy said. "If we bark in the woods, no dog will hear us, only the trees. But..." an idea occurred to her. "Maybe the wasp will hear me. Maybe he'll come and help again. He could find the police dogs and pass the message on! Why didn't I think of that before?"

"Maybe," Petra agreed, "but if you go up the bank, it comes to the edge of some fields. Go in the field and bark from there. Our village isn't far away. I'm sure some dog will hear you."

Lucy looked uncertainly at the steep wooded bank beside the track. Petra often disappeared into the trees to look for deer, but Lucy never did. The steep bank was full of snapped branches, tree trunks, bracken, stinging nettles, long grass and thorny brambles. Somehow Petra could leap through and over all the obstacles on the forest floor without being held back, though she usually came back covered in thorns that the Daleys had to pull out of her. Petra didn't seem to mind. In fact, she loved it, but it wasn't Lucy's cup of tea. She wasn't as young or as athletic as the pointer and preferred to stay on the footpath with the Daleys.

She didn't want to go, and in normal times she'd have refused, but it wasn't normal times and she knew she had to do everything she could to help.

"Are you with me Bella?" she asked the young dog who was walking beside her, "you'll probably be quicker than me in getting up there to the fields at the top."

"I'm ready," she replied, a knowing look on her face.

"Then let's go." Lucy casually stopped at the side of the track, pretending to sniff a pine cone. Bella took the hint and stopped to sniff as well. The Daleys were deep in conversation and Petra pulled on the lead, keeping them moving forward. Lucy knew they wouldn't look back, as she always stopped to sniff things and never ran off like Petra did. They wouldn't be worried.

Petra kept the Daleys moving on while Lucy and Bella began picking their way through the undergrowth as they negotiated the slope.

"Ow!" said Lucy as she felt brambles pulling at her skin.

"Ouch!" cried Bella, as nettles under her feet stung the skin between her toes.

Petra is crazy to choose to come running about in all of this, and enjoy it, thought Lucy as she struggled to push through the mass of brambles and long grass. Hating every minute, the two Dalmatians pressed on up the slope. Their progress was slow and they could hear the Daleys shouting their names, having realised they were both missing. Lucy would have loved to return to them, knowing how worried they'd be about the constant disappearance of their dogs, but she fought her instinct of loyalty to her humans and battled on. They would have to wait a few more minutes.

At last, the slope levelled out, and through the trees, Lucy could make out a fence with grazing cows in the field beyond. The two dogs entered the field and looked at each other, uncertain who was going to do the barking.

"It was your idea," Lucy said to Bella, "and you've been in the puppy farm. You're the best one to do it, if you're happy to? I'll see if I can call my old wasp friend while you're busy."

Bella stood a little taller, proud that the older dog trusted her with this important task. She knew that Lucy had doubted her yesterday, so it meant a lot to her that she'd changed her mind. Facing the cows, who looked up, startled, she began.

***

"Where have you two been?" Mrs Daley exclaimed later, when Lucy and Bella returned to them, covered in thorns. "I'm going to have to keep you all on the lead forever more - you keep taking it in turns to vanish. If it's not Petra, it's you two. You're going to turn my hair grey, making me worry like that."

"I think we'd better look into getting them all one of those tracking collars, so we can see where they are if they do disappear," said Mr Daley.

"Yes, good idea. In the meantime, they're all staying on their leads," Mrs Daley replied, clipping Lucy and Bella on and heading back along the track towards home.

"How did you get on?" Petra asked, as the three dogs walked side by side, Bella limping slightly as her paws were throbbing from the nettle stings.

"Good, I think," Lucy replied. "I don't think our wasp will get my message. I only saw one wasp in the field and it seemed pretty sleepy. There aren't many flowers about now for them, so they might be less energetic. Bella did well though, in asking for news and giving some more information about the farm's location. We heard from an Irish Setter and a Labrador. They said the message had been passed right down the county last night and received by a police dog who recognised the descriptions. He's going to -"

"*A* police dog? *One* dog?" asked Petra. "I thought we were trying to get the message to a squad of police dogs?"

"If you'll let me finish..." Lucy tutted at Petra's impatience. "We've found out that police dogs don't live in kennels all together like we imagined. They live with their human officer. The one I'm talking about - Police Dog Blake - is a German Shepherd, and he lives with PD Willow, a springer spaniel who's a sniffer dog. It's Willow's job to find things."

"Blake said he'd take charge of the situation and get those dogs found!" Bella added, her tail whipping back and forth in excitement. "My plan worked!"

"Yes," said Lucy. "It looks like it, but let's not celebrate until we know for sure. We'll have to wait and trust that Blake and Willow can do it. It's a tough mission. They've not only got to find the farm; they've got to make their human understand what's happening too." Lucy didn't want to be pessimistic, but she knew it was important not to get their hopes up too soon. The police dogs had a lot to do and there was no guarantee of success.

Lucy, Petra and Bella walked the Daleys home, all three of them thinking of the dogs trapped in the puppy farm. All they could do now was wait.

FOUR

There was nothing on the news that night. Or the next night. Desperate to know what was happening, the dogs tried barking to see if they could get any updates, but it was impossible as now all three were confined to leads on walks. Being stuck so close to the Daleys on the morning walk meant they were mostly out of range for receiving messages from other dogs. It was so frustrating not being able to hear anything. The three of them pulled like steam trains on their leads, attempting to drag the Daleys into positions where they could make out what dogs in the distance were trying to tell them.

It didn't work. The Daleys got so sick of having their arms pulled out of their sockets, they ended the walk early and turned for home.

"We can't have this forever," Mrs Daley complained, thinking the dogs were pulling because they wanted to run. "If we can't let them off their leads to burn off their energy, we're going to end up with stretched arms, like cooked spaghetti."

"Yes," Mr Daley agreed. "I'll look into those tracking collars I mentioned. We need to let them off, but we want to know where they are too, since they've decided to take it in turns to go missing."

Lucy, Petra and Bella spent the rest of the day in the house. The Daleys both went to work, and the dogs had nothing to do but wait. They tried sleeping to pass the time. They gnawed on their chews. Lucy gave Petra and Bella's faces a good wash. Petra stood up on her hind legs and put her front paws on the kitchen worktops to see if there were any breakfast scraps left she could eat. Bella tried to tell some jokes, but no-one was in the mood for them.

The day passed so slowly. There was a moment's excitement when they were startled by the sound of the letterbox rattling, followed by the thud of the post as it landed on the mat. The dogs sprang from their beds and barked loudly at the intrusion as was their daily routine. Once that task was out of the way, they all went back to bed, ready to resume their doze.

'Zzzzz.' Lucy heard a sound and lifted her head, ears pricked to locate the source. It seemed to be coming from the doormat. She frowned. *How could the post be humming?* She wondered if she'd imagined it, but Petra and Bella were also looking with confusion at the brown and white envelopes lying on the mat in front of the door.

"Do letters usually buzz?" Bella asked.

Lucy didn't reply, but she stood and hesitantly moved towards the pile of letters. She lowered her head to sniff the top envelope.

"Don't stand on me, pleazzz," a tiny, dry voice rasped. Lucy recognised it at once.

"Wasp! You're here! But are you alright? You don't look well." The wasp was clinging onto the corner of an envelope and didn't look sleek and waspy like she remembered. He seemed … shrivelled somehow.

"I'm near the end I'm afraid, my lady, but I heard you'd been looking for me again, so I wanted to come and say goodbye. I can't help you this time. I'm sorry."

"Hello, wasp," Petra greeted her old friend who'd been her guide to the puppy farm. "It's good to see you again. What do you mean, 'near the end' and 'goodbye'?"

"And how did you get in here?" Bella asked a question that hadn't occurrzd to Lucy and Petra.

"So many questionzzz," the wasp replied in a whisper. "I hitched a ride though the letterbox on a letter. I thought I might get squashed as the man pushed me through, but there was nothing to lose, so I thought I might as well try to see you one last time."

"Why is it the last time?" Lucy asked.

"My time is up," he said sadly. "Winter is coming. It's the end for uzzz. We can't survive through the cold monthzzz."

"What? No!" Lucy was aghast. "It can't be. You can hibernate. I've seen it on the TV. Lots of creatures do it. They go into a very deep sleep over the winter months and wake up again in the spring."

"The queen hibernatezzz," the wasp replied, "but not us worker waspzzz. We only live one season. I wanted to tell you both that I am so pleased to have met you and been able to assist you. Maybe when I'm gone, you'll be able to spread the word about how waspzzz are not the enemy. Tell every dog you meet that we are good and helpful creaturezzz."

Tears pricked at Lucy's eyes. "I will not," she said, "because you're not going anywhere, except into hibernation. Help me," she said to Petra and Bella.

Between the three of them, Lucy, Petra and Bella set up Operation Hibernation. Lucy opened the kitchen door to let them all into the rest of the house. Petra stole a sock that Mr Daley had left on a radiator to dry and Bella carried the envelope with the wasp still clinging to the edge. All three went upstairs into a spare bedroom and prepared a space under the bed for the wasp's winter slumber. Petra placed the sock in a dark corner under the bed and Bella shook the envelope gently so that the wasp fell onto the sock. Tenderly, Lucy wrapped the sock around the wasp so he'd be warm and placed an apple she'd taken from the fruit bowl beside him.

"So you have something to eat if you wake up before spring," she said.

"You're so kind, all of you," the wasp sighed, snuggling into his sock.

"It's the least we could do, after what you've done for us," Petra said. "This is our chance to say thank you."

The dogs backed out of the bedroom and returned to the kitchen, Lucy closing all the doors behind them so it would look like they'd been there all along.

When they heard a key being inserted into the front door later on, and Mrs Daley entered the kitchen, the dogs jumped all over her to show her how pleased they were that she was home and what a boring, uneventful day they'd had. Lucy and Bella wrinkled up their noses in big smiles, and Petra wagged her tail in circles like the propeller of an aeroplane.

"Hello, girls, are you pleased to see me?" Mrs Daley chuckled. "You need a walk, but there's no way I can manage all three of you on the lead on my own.

I'll get dragged about like I'm on water skis. Let's go to the beach."

Lucy, Petra and Bella all piled into the back of Mrs Daley's car and she drove them to the nearby beach. Having been in the house all day, they were all so full of energy and couldn't help but enjoy a play on the sand. The puppy farm and the wasp were forgotten for a moment as the sea-smelling air filled their nostrils and the wide-open beach called to them. They chased each other, played leap-frog, ran in the water lapping the shore and dug holes in the sand until their hearts were pounding and their tongues were hanging out. Before they got a chance to attempt any barking, they found themselves being clipped on their leads and taken back to the car. The light was fading already.

"Come on, pups, let's get back for some tea," Mrs Daley said, pulling her coat tightly around her to block the chilly coastal wind. Autumn was ending and the arrival of winter could be felt in the bite of the breeze and the hasty departure of the sun.

Feeling guilty for enjoying themselves rather than trying to find out some news, the dogs reluctantly came away from the beach and jumped back into the car.

"We shouldn't have been playing," Lucy said. Her head hung low. "We should have been thinking about those poor dogs who are locked up and need help. We should have been trying to find out what's happening."

"I think we will find out," said Bella. "I've just got a feeling it will be tonight. I'll have to try not to fall asleep later when the news is on. I don't want to miss it."

Lucy and Petra looked at the young dog. Could she be right? They had no idea how she could know that, but they knew better than to ignore the young Dalmatian. With hope filling their hearts, the dogs looked forward to getting back home and waiting for good news.

FIVE

First, there was something about a hospital, then some local politics, then details about a proposed new bypass that lots of people were objecting to. Several more stories flashed across the screen, but nothing about dogs. Crammed together on the sofa in between the Daleys, Lucy, Petra and Bella had been watching the TV screen intently since the news came on. Lucy and Petra grew anxious. The story they were waiting for wasn't there. They both looked at Bella, sandwiched in the middle, but the young dog didn't appear worried.

"And finally." the newsreader began, reaching the last story of the programme, "we have some more news for you of dogs behaving strangely."

Lucy, Petra and Bella's ears pricked at the mention of dogs and they all leaned forward slightly.

The Daleys didn't notice. They were giving all of their attention to the TV, too.

"Last week we brought you the story of a group of dogs crossing Windermere Lake in a boat ... being pushed through the water by two dogs swimming alongside it," the newsreader said. The screen changed, showing an image of the rowing boat. It was dark but still clear to see that it was carrying a crew of assorted dogs. Petra blinked rapidly as she noticed herself in the water beside the boat. It was so strange to see herself on the television.

"Ohh, there's Petra!" Mrs Daley squeaked, even though she'd already seen the video of the dogs-in-the-boat last week.

"It was believed this was a daring escape mission," the newsreader went on, "by dogs who had been stolen from their homes and were seeking their way back to their families. This pointer seemed to be leading the way." Another image appeared, showing the dogs walking along the country road through the small village. Petra was in the lead.

"The dogs were almost re-captured by the thieves, who tracked them using a drone, but the men gave up after suffering a surprise wasp attack. Helpful members of the public attempted to stop them from escaping but the thieves fled across the fields and have evaded capture ... until today."

Unable to contain their excitement, all three dogs slid off the sofa and stood on the carpet in front of the TV so they could see it better.

"Awww, come on girls," Mr Daley complained, "I can't see the screen with your three bums in the way!"

Lucy and Petra lay down but didn't take their eyes off the screen. Bella remained standing as the details of the thieves' capture unfolded.

"This morning, PC Graham Daniels found that his dogs, PDs Blake and Willow were acting strangely. He knew their behaviour was out of character and that they must be trying to tell him something. So, he listened. Zoe Day has the details."

The screen switched to an image of a black-haired female reporter interviewing the policeman. His two dogs were by his side.

"That's them!" Bella barked. "It's Blake and Willow."

"Shhhhh," said the Daleys, who were on the ends of their seats now.

"Can you tell us what happened this morning, officer, and how your dogs helped in the capture of notorious dog thieves?" the reporter asked.

The policeman explained how the dogs' odd behaviour started straight away that morning when he took them for a walk. "We were actually meant to be off duty today," he explained. "But the dogs both started pulling awfully on their leads as soon as we left the house. They don't normally do that unless they're working and want to show me something, so I decided to see if that's what they were trying to do."

He went on to say how the dogs took him on a route he'd never been before. It certainly wasn't somewhere he'd taken them on a walk, so he had no idea where they were going or how they knew where to go. They took him over fields and through woods until finally they arrived at a small compound surrounded by a metal fence. Once there, they stopped and growled.

"I knew there was something wrong with the place," PC Daniels said. "The way it was hidden away -

I didn't even know it existed - and the fact the metal fence was also lined with panels so you couldn't see what was inside was suspicious. Plus, the dogs had led me there, so I knew they were trying to tell me something. I phoned my station to let them know and soon the place was surrounded by police."

The screen changed again to show footage of the police breaking into the compound by cutting through the chains wrapped around the entrance gates. There was no Buster and Baxter to keep intruders out now so once the chains fell, it was easy for them to march in.

The thieves were seen trying to run away and escape again but they were quickly brought down by Blake, who pounced on one of them while another police dog who'd been brought along – a Belgian Malinois – grabbed the other one. The two men were shown being led away, hand-cuffed and put into police cars.

The newsreader appeared again. "The police recovered twenty-two dogs and puppies from a building on the site," he said. "Four of the dogs were in very poor condition, and all had litters of puppies with them. The men arrested had clearly been running a puppy farm. All of them, including four more dogs, believed to have been stolen just days ago, have been taken away by the RSPCA, who will treat the animals and attempt to trace their owners. Meanwhile, the men responsible for the suffering of these dogs face up to five years in prison due to the new Animal Welfare Bill that has just come into force. Thanks to PDs Blake and Willow, plus their human police colleagues, it is hoped that these two men will now be brought to justice and pay the consequences for their crimes."

There were wild celebrations in the Daley household as the news ended and the weather forecast came on. Mr and Mrs Daley were hugging each other and Lucy, Petra and Bella jumped all over them on the sofa.

"Oww!" they cried as three whip-like wagging tails whacked them repeatedly. "What's got into you three?" The three dogs were so hysterical, the Daleys put them out into the back garden to run off their sudden bout of energy. They whizzed around the garden like maniacs and the Daleys laughed, watching them.

"I've said it before – I'm sure those dogs understand everything that's said. It's like they've just watched the news and now they're celebrating," said Mr Daley.

"Don't be silly dear," said Mrs Daley. "Dogs don't watch the news."

SIX

Lucy, Petra and Bella were happy for life to go back to normal. There was nothing for them to worry about anymore. They were safe and all the dogs and puppies from the puppy farm had been rescued. They'd be returned to their owners when found. If not, loving new homes with kind, caring humans would take them in to restart their lives.

The three dogs snuggled happily together in the kitchen that night, content that they'd played their part in the rescue even though they couldn't actually be there.

"It's just as well you could remember the route so well and describe the landmarks you'd seen near the farm," Lucy remarked to Petra as they lay in their beds. "That's what made Blake and Willow able to guide their human and find the right place. And there they were, the bad men, all ready to be caught."

"I wasn't sure they'd go back," said Petra. "That's why I was so worried about the dogs we left behind. But at least the thieves had returned to look after the ones they still had."

"Don't be silly Petra," Bella said quietly, remembering her time in what she now knew was the puppy farm. "The men didn't go back out of concern for the dogs. They went back to get it going again. In just a few days, they'd already stolen four more dogs. All they wanted to do was keep breeding and selling more and more puppies. They didn't care about them at all. They just wanted to make money."

"Yes, well, that's all over now, thanks to you two," Lucy said, trying to lift the mood. "Between you, you've stopped their greedy, cruel activities and hopefully they'll never be able to do it again. You should be proud of yourselves."

They all stopped talking to take in Lucy's words and picture the rescued dogs, who they knew would now be sleeping with full bellies, clean, warm and safe. Gradually, they drifted off to sleep too, looking forward to the peaceful days ahead.

The days ahead were anything but peaceful, though. The phone started ringing the next morning and didn't stop. The Daleys took turns answering it.

"Who was that one?" Mrs Daley asked as her husband put the handset down at lunchtime.

"It was a producer from 'Sunrise!'. They saw the news last night and want to do an interview with us and PC Daniels, plus Petra, Blake and Willow. We'll have to go to London!"

"Oh gosh," said Mrs Daley as the phone started ringing again.

"That was Dogs Are Go. They've seen the news too, plus they've watched some of our videos of Petra on the internet. They're creating a new canine energy drink and they want to use Petra in their advertising campaign. This is crazy! Petra's going to be famous."

"We'll have two famous dogs," said Mr Daley, looking at Lucy and Petra. "We'll end up being their agents, taking bookings for them and chauffeuring them to their engagements."

Mrs Daley laughed as the phone rang yet again.

Petra gulped. This was what she'd wanted. It was the reason she'd been so keen to rescue Gomez and Gizmo when they were stolen. Although she loved Lucy, she'd been getting fed up with being ignored and pushed aside by people desperate to meet her famous friend. She'd wanted to be noticed, too. Petra had craved fame and glory. But now it was happening, she wasn't sure she wanted it anymore. What Petra really wanted was to go back to a normal, quiet life just going for walks and chasing rabbits. No more adventures. But it didn't look like that was going to happen.

Be careful what you wish for, Petra told herself.

"That was the village primary school," Mrs Daley said, putting the phone down again. "They're doing some work on local heroes and they'd like to have Petra in for their assembly on Friday as she's a local hero. I've said yes. That'll be a nice little local event to start off with before some of these bigger things. And Lucy can go with her as she's also a hero for the work she does to help Peregrine Pets find new homes for rescued and unwanted animals."

"Yes," Mr Daley agreed. "It'll be a nice introduction for Petra to start meeting her adoring public. Sounds like she's going to have to get used to it. She's a dog in demand."

"Hmm, I think our lives are about to change," Mrs Daley said, "having two famous dogs. I just hope poor Bella doesn't feel left out. I asked the school if she could come along too, just so she doesn't have to be left behind on her own. I don't like to think of her being by herself, not knowing where we've gone. After the bad start she had, I think it would worry her."

Bella didn't mind being left out at all. She was just happy she'd come to live with such a wonderful family. She got all the attention she wanted now. She needed nothing else.

SEVEN

Over the next few days, a number of TV shows called to book Petra for interviews. Mr and Mrs Daley accepted them all. "If it helps to let more people know about puppy farms, that can only be a good thing," Mrs Daley said, "and any money we're paid can be donated to Dog Lost."

There was also the dog food company who wanted Petra to appear in a commercial to advertise their energy drink, and a games company who wanted to make a computer game based on her. Petra was indeed a dog in demand!

Before these, though, was the school visit.

"What's a school?" Petra asked Lucy a couple of days before they were due to appear. Lucy had always been a wise dog, but since she'd discovered the television news, she'd taken to watching all sorts of programmes with interest. Since she understood almost everything people said, she was learning lots from them.

"It's a place where young humans go to learn things," Lucy said. "Where the adults train them."

"Oh," said Petra, "like puppy class?" She thought back to how she'd gone to classes with the Daleys to learn how to sit, stay, give a paw, fetch a ball and walk on the lead. She was also supposed to have learned how to socialise nicely with the other puppies, but she'd been a bit too exuberant playing with some of them and struggled with that part.

"A bit," said Lucy. "Though I think they learn different things at school than we do at puppy class."

"Sounds like fun," said Petra, imagining all the pats and belly rubs she'd get from the children.

"Yes, but you'll have to stay calm," Lucy warned. "You can't go whacking about like you normally do, whipping everyone with your tail. Some of the children will only be small and you could knock them right over. You need to be careful."

"I will."

Since returning from her escape from the puppy farm, Petra tried to be a bit less 'crazy pointer' than she had been before. Since the dog thieves had been arrested, the Daleys had relaxed and started letting them all off their leads again. Petra tried to be more considerate to stop the Daleys worrying about where she was. She still couldn't resist disappearing into the woods on walks. As soon as she caught the scent of a rabbit or deer, it pulled her after it like a gravitational force. But now, she regularly returned to the track to show the Daleys she was still with them, before vanishing back into the undergrowth. Lucy and Bella always stayed on the track with the Daleys, so there was no more mention of tracking collars for them. Things were returning to normal.

Soon it was Friday and time to visit the school. Mr Daley was at work so Mrs Daley had all three dogs to manage on her own.

"Oh, don't worry about that," the cheerful headmistress said when Mrs Daley explained the problem. "I'm sure I can find a couple of pupils who can help to hold them for you."

"Are you sure? They're very strong dogs."

"Oh yes, I know just who to ask!"

The assembly began. Mrs Daley sat with Petra, waiting for her turn, while two pupils sat beside her, delighted to be picked to hold onto Lucy and Bella. Lucy was on her best behaviour for her young handler, Daisy. She knew how to present herself in public. But

Bella was very excited and couldn't sit still. She saw all the children sitting on the floor of the hall and was desperate to meet them all. She was such a fidget, the teacher of the boy who was trying to keep hold of her whispered that it would probably be best if he took her outside on the grassed area of the playground. He quietly slipped off his chair and headed out of the hall, taking the wildly wagging Bella with him.

Petra did her best to keep still while she waited for her turn. They were the last ones to be introduced. Before that, they listened to a firewoman, a paramedic and a farmer, then there was a man who'd rescued a boy from drowning, a girl who'd had all her long hair cut off for charity and a couple who'd been running a local youth club in the town for the last 30 years. Then it was Petra and Lucy's turn.

Mrs Daley stepped up to the front of the hall and blushed at all the faces staring back. Petra looked up at her. She should have been talking, telling the children about why Petra and Lucy were heroes, but she seemed to have got stage fright. She couldn't speak. Lucy also noticed, from where she was standing at the front of the hall, held by the girl, Daisy. Realising Mrs Daley needed some help, Lucy performed one of her tricks. She stood up, dropped her left shoulder and did a forward roll right in front of the smallest children who were sitting in the front row.

The silence was broken. The children roared with laughter and clapped in delight. Lucy gave a modest bow, then sat back down, looking up at Mrs Daley, who was also laughing. Now much more relaxed, Mrs Daley could tell the children all about the two dogs and what they'd done to be local heroes. "We're hoping that Petra won't need to be rescued or lead any more rescues in the future," she said at the end, "but Lucy here will continue her work with the local animal rescue centre,

Peregrine Pets, so you may see her at some of their events if you go along."

After a big round of applause, which made Mrs Daley blush even more, a teacher escorted the children out of the hall a class at a time. Many of them hung back to give Lucy and Petra a pat on their way back to their classrooms, and the two dogs accepted them patiently.

"Well done," Lucy said to Petra for keeping still and not knocking any of the smaller children over.

When all the younger classes had gone, the last ones to leave were the oldest. When they left to head back to their room, Daisy didn't know what to do. She was still holding onto Lucy's lead. She needed to hand her back over to Mrs Daley, but she was distracted, talking with the other heroes from the assembly. Daisy didn't want to interrupt, so she took Lucy back to class with her. Her friends would love to have a Dalmatian in their next lesson with them!

By the time Mrs Daley finished chatting and was ready to go home, she looked around to find there was no sign of Bella or Lucy, only Petra, who stood next to her on the lead she was holding.

"Where are those two Dallies at?" she said, looking worriedly all around her. "They've disappeared! Oh, not again. My nerves can't take this. Mrs Cross!" she called after the headmistress who was guiding the visitors back to reception. "My dogs are missing!"

EIGHT

"How did it go at the school? Were they impressed with our heroes, or heroines, I should say?" Mr Daley asked later when he arrived home from work.

Mrs Daley plonked herself on the sofa with a cup of tea and let out a long breath. "Yes, the assembly went well," she replied, "and the children seemed to love Lucy and Petra, but..."

"Oh - a but. Nothing's ever without drama, is it?" Mr Daley kicked off his shoes and sat down next to his wife, placing his cup on the coffee table.

"After the assembly, I got talking to the other people who were there to speak. I had Petra with me. Lucy and Bella were with a couple of pupils Mrs Cross had chosen as they were used to dogs. The girl who had Lucy, Daisy, has a pointer like Petra. He's called Otto. Anyway," she said, returning to the story, "when

I finished chatting and went to leave the school, there was no sign of Lucy and Bella. The kids had gone back to class, and those two had gone too. I had no idea where they were."

Mr Daley smiled. He could imagine, after recent events, how this would have panicked his wife, but he knew the story ended well as all three dogs were in their beds in the kitchen. He'd just been bowled over by them all when he came in the front door. Knowing they were all safe and sound meant he could relax as he listened to the story.

"Mrs Cross took me to the Year 6 classroom first to find Daisy and Lucy. They were getting art equipment out for their next lesson. Daisy was there, but not Lucy. Mrs Cross asked her where Lucy was and she looked around, expecting to see her. 'She was just here a moment ago,' she said. Mrs Cross wasn't very pleased and had a few words with her about responsibility, but you could see the girl had only turned her back for a minute. She thought Lucy was still in the room. So, that meant Lucy was AWOL and I had a pretty good idea where she might be found."

Mr Daley smiled, imagining what he thought was going to happen next.

"And I was right. We left the classroom and bumped right into a dinner lady who had Lucy with her. Of course, she'd found her way into the kitchen, hadn't she? Managed to scoff a tray of cheese flan before anyone saw her. I was mortified! Fortunately, Mrs Cross saw the funny side, but I'm not sure the dinner lady did." Mrs Daley blew on her tea and took a small sip before she told the second part of the story.

"That's exactly what I was thinking," chuckled Mr Daley. "If there's ever any doubt where Lucy Leopard is, check the kitchen! And what about Jingle Bella? Where was she hiding?"

***

Mr Daley loved coming up with silly names for the dogs, and they all had several each. Jingle Bella had been one of the first one given to Bella. When she'd come to live with them, they'd discovered that she wasn't fully house trained and sometimes had accidents. They never told her off or punished her, but encouraged her to ask to go out into the back garden when she needed to 'do her business'. Bella quickly caught on to this and, wanting to please her new family, whenever she needed to go out, she'd use her nose to jingle the keys that hung in the lock of the back door. "Listen to her, jingling the keys," Mrs Daley had said. "It's like she's a rich person ringing a bell for service and we, her staff, have been summoned!" She was only joking, as they were both impressed with the young dog's intelligence, but of course, it had inspired Mr Daley's love of creating new names. Jingle Bella came first, swiftly followed by Jingle Bells and Ding Dong Bells.

***

"Mrs Cross took me to another classroom where a boy called Rohan was. He'd been given Bella to look after, but she couldn't settle in the hall with all the children, so he'd taken her outside on the grass. Mrs Cross assumed he must have taken her back to class with him, but again, when we got there, Bella wasn't there.

"His teacher asked him where she was and he said he'd asked another pupil to hold on to her while he went to the toilet. When he'd come back, they were all going back to their classrooms, and he forgot. So, we went to all the other classrooms...and she wasn't in any of them. I was getting worried she might have got out, but Mrs Cross said she couldn't have as all the gates out onto the roads, front and back, were locked. We checked the kitchen, the toilets, cloakrooms, everywhere. Then Mrs Cross wondered if a member of staff might have taken her to the staff room, so we headed there. To get to the staff room, we had to walk through the library...and that's where she was!"

"In the library? What was she doing? Reading *The Hundred and One Dalmatians*?"

"Ha ha, nearly. She was lying down being read to, actually." Mrs Daley smiled as she remembered the vision of the young dog lying on her back next to a small child. The child was stroking Bella's tummy with one hand while reading a book to her at the same time. Bella was clearly loving it. "The teacher with the children said she'd come bowling in, wiggling and smiling, 'Bella bombed' them all, licking their ears, then she'd settled down and had a big fuss made. She'd totally distracted them from their reading, so the teacher had the idea they could all take turns to read their story to her. And that's what they were doing when I found her."

"Hmmm, Bella the library dog?" Mr Daley's mind was working, wondering how he could turn that into a new nickname. "Well, we have said she's a clever girl. Maybe she'll be learning to read next!"

"Yes dear, don't get carried away. So, Mrs Cross apologised that the pupils had been a bit remiss in their care of the dogs, but it was fine. I just hope LuLu isn't sick later after eating all that cheese flan."

Mr Daley drank the rest of his tea and stood up, ready to change out of his work clothes. "I'm glad it went well, though I'm not sure the school will invite them back in the future after Lucy raided the kitchen and Bella stormed the library. At least Petra didn't cause any trouble."

"Yes," said Mrs Daley, "I think you're probably right about that."

NINE

They were wrong. The following Monday, the Daleys' phone rang, and it was the school. Mrs Cross said that following Bella's impromptu library visit, the pupils had been asking when she was coming back so they could read to her again.

"Some of the children lack confidence with reading and are getting some extra help, but many of them don't enjoy reading aloud," Mrs Cross told Mrs Daley. "But on Friday, when Bella turned up in the library, Mr Green said he'd never seen the children more engaged. They all wanted a turn at reading to Bella, and having her there made them much more relaxed. Probably because Bella just listened and didn't correct them. We'd love to have her back again to be our library mascot. I think the pupils would fall over themselves to come and do some reading if Bella was their audience. What do you think?"

"I'm very surprised, actually," Mrs Daley replied honestly. "Bella is only young and quite high energy. I wouldn't have thought she'd be calm enough to sit still and listen to children read. I have heard of reading dogs in schools, and I know there are a number of charities who offer this, with trained dogs. Bella hasn't had any training, though. I'm not sure she's suitable."

"I understand," said Mrs Cross, "but the children really loved her and are asking if she's coming back. We could try it and see how it goes?"

So, it was agreed that Bella would return for another visit. The Daleys thought that as Lucy often had things to do in connection with her being the face of the local animal rescue and re-homing centre, and now Petra had engagements too, it would be nice for Bella to have something of her own to do.

And that's what they did. Mrs Daley felt like her dogs' secretary and chauffeur. She was always driving them around to different events and interviews.

In no time, Bella became a valued member of the school team and even had her photo on their website as Bella the Reading Dog. As Mrs Cross had predicted, the children couldn't wait to get to their library to see Bella and there were always lots of volunteers to read to her. Where some children hadn't liked reading before, now a session of 'read with Bella' was used as a reward. When she knew she was going to school, Bella pulled on her lead and couldn't wait to get in. The pupils were all used to being 'Bella bombed' when they first met her, as she was so enthusiastic and pleased to see them, but surprisingly this didn't frighten any of them. It had the opposite effect and Mrs Cross reported that interacting with Bella had made a lot of pupils much more confident. "She's the star of the school," she said one day, sending Bella home with a gold star stuck to her collar.

Lucy also continued to impress in her fundraising work for Peregrine Pets. Whenever she was present at their events, more money was raised than when she wasn't there. She'd gone to their Halloween event, partnering a staff member dressed as Cruella de'Vil and she'd been part of their 'Fearful Fireworks' programme in November, touring around local schools to spread the message about how to help pets cope with Bonfire Night, which was often distressing and caused some dogs and cats to run away from their homes in terror.

Now that Christmas was approaching, Lucy was going to be helping them with their Puppy Present campaign to try and stop people giving puppies as Christmas presents, thinking they'd be cute and cuddly like teddy bears. The charity always received lots of unwanted puppies in January when people discovered how much hard work they were, and how they hadn't really known what a puppy would need. Peregrine Pets did as much as they could to educate people about the responsibility of owning a dog and in November and December they toured schools, with Lucy helping to demonstrate their message.

That left Petra. She'd accompanied the Daleys on some interviews for local TV news, been to London to appear on a morning show and had lots of photographs taken for a variety of magazines. Petra had been tentatively looking forward to them. When she'd rescued the stolen dogs, getting famous had been part of her incentive, although she'd later changed her priorities and learned that friendship was far more important than fame. But she'd liked the feeling of being wanted, and getting booked to appear in magazines, adverts and TV programmes made her feel important.

She'd been nervous about her first job, but Bella went with her to her first photoshoot. Petra had thought this was just to prevent Bella having to be left home alone, since Lucy was with Mrs Daley doing something with Peregrine Pets, but when they got to the place, there had been a big surprise waiting for her. All the dogs she'd rescued from the puppy farm were there too.

Buster and Baxter were with their new owner, a giant of a man with a big bushy red beard. He was like the human equivalent of his dogs. The others too: Pepper, Dusty, Storm, Sprite, Gomez and Gizmo were all there for the reunion.

The photographer rolled his eyes and tutted. He hated working with animals. With human models, he could tell them what to do and they'd do it, but animals did the opposite. It made taking a decent picture almost impossible.

It was a good story: all the dogs who'd been stolen and escaped together being reunited for a picture to go with the tale of their adventure, but he knew there was no chance of getting the dogs nice and calm and onto set quickly for the pictures. As soon as they saw each other, they went crazy, wagging their tails and jumping all over each other. They were all so pleased to be back together again, they couldn't contain their excitement.

He threw his hands in the air and went to get a coffee. There was no chance of getting a good picture while they were like this. It would just be a blur.

"Call me when they've calmed down," he told his flustered young assistant, thrusting the camera into his hands and stalking off.

TEN

"I think we've got a problem," Mr Daley said later to Mrs Daley. He'd taken the dogs to Petra's first photoshoot by himself, since Lucy and Mrs Daley had been busy elsewhere.

"What's that?" she asked, putting their plates on the table and sitting down to eat.

"Er...well, it seems Petra is camera shy."

"Camera shy? How can a dog be camera shy?" she scoffed, biting a piece of broccoli off her fork.

"She won't look at the camera. At all. She looks down or away when the camera is on her. She won't look at it."

Mrs Daley frowned, so he described the day.

Eventually, after all the dogs had greeted each other and shared their news, they'd settled enough for the anxious assistant to call the photographer back in. He'd appeared, looking slightly calmer after his coffee, and explained what he wanted.

A rowing boat was set up in the centre of the room with a variety of blue linens arranged on the floor around it to replicate water. There were screens behind the boat showing trees, mountains, and a dark, moonlit sky filled with glimmering stars. The photographer wanted to replicate the now well-known boat scene shown on news channels around the country where the dogs had sailed across Windermere Lake, powered by Petra and Pepper, who had pushed it from behind. The photographer wanted all the dogs in the same positions they'd been in on the night. He even had a skateboard propped up in the back. After a bit of shuffling and arranging, the dogs were where they needed to be. Their owners helped keep them in their positions while the photographer got his camera ready. Bella loved being up at the front of the boat, in her lookout position. She pushed her shoulders back, and stretched out, looking sleek and streamlined, waiting for the picture to be taken. Petra and Pepper stood at the back of the boat. At first, they'd been directed to lie down, so it looked as if they were swimming behind the boat, as they had done on the night in question, but the photographer declared he couldn't see them well enough so they needed to be standing up.

"Right, that's it. That's the shot right there." The photographer framed the image with his hands, before backing away, clicking his fingers at the assistant to pass him his camera. "Look this way, doggies," he said, lifting the camera to his face and clicking his tongue. Behind him, the assistant jumped up and down, making a gobbling noise, like a turkey, to get the dogs to look towards the camera.

Bella stood up even straighter, her front paws on the prow of the boat, and looked right into the camera like a professional model. Just like Lucy, she seemed to know all about having her picture taken and loved it, striking a pose to show herself off to her best. The other dogs also responded to the assistant's odd behaviour and the strange noise he was making. Dusty the greyhound cocked her head, wondering what on earth he was doing.

Petra, too, looked towards the camera until she saw its big, black round lens staring back at her like a huge unblinking eye. Like a deep, dark, hole. Like a trap. The memory of falling through the rotten wood and into a bottomless pit leapt into Petra's mind and shook her like an earthquake. She would have died down in that hole if Lucy hadn't found her and worked a miracle to get her out. She'd have been there forever. Petra blinked and lowered her head. She couldn't bear to look at the dark, round lens. It felt like it was going to suck her into it and keep her prisoner where no-one would find her. Ever.

The photographer clicked away, getting his pictures, until he noticed Petra, looking at the floor.

"Dog at the back!" he yelled. The young assistant whispered the correct name to him, knowing which dog he meant, and the photographer echoed it loudly. "Petra! Look at the camera, there's a good doggy."

But Petra wouldn't. No matter what anyone did, or what attention-getting sounds they made, Petra would not look at the camera.

"Give me strength!" the photographer roared, checking his watch in frustration. "I haven't got time for doggy divas." To solve the problem, he switched Pepper and Petra around so that Pepper was closest to the camera and took his pictures with her in the forefront while Petra hid behind her.

"She's still got the energy drink for dogs advert to film, and the game company who want to meet her regarding the video game they're making about her. She's not going to do very well at either of those if she's suddenly decided she's shy," Mr Daley said.

"It doesn't sound like our Meister," said Mrs Daley, using one of her husband's nicknames for Petra. "She's always been such a confident dog. Maybe it was because all the other dogs were there – they could have put her off somehow. Hopefully she'll be fine when she's on her own with no distractions."

"Yes, I hope so too," Mr Daley agreed. "These companies are expecting an action-packed, adventuring, full-of-energy type of dog, not one that hides away behind others. I don't want to waste their time or their money if she's not going to do what they've booked her for."

Later, when the dogs were alone in the kitchen and discussing their days, Petra confessed, "I used to be jealous of you, Lucy, when you started getting all that attention and having your picture taken all the time. I wanted that too. I wanted to be known and to have people asking to take my picture, but now it's happening, I don't like it. It makes me feel trapped."

"That's probably because you're The Poltermeist," Lucy said, wise as ever. "Your skills are in being invisible, staying out of sight, like a ghost. It's what you were bred for. It's who you are. Don't feel bad or jealous about not enjoying being the centre of attention. It isn't you."

"But you and Bella both love it," said Petra, feeling like the odd dog out.

"Yes, but we were bred to be noticed. That's why we look like we do. We're meant to stand out. We can't hide away, but we don't mind. Don't try to be like us;

be yourself. Everyone knows you led those dogs to safety. That took bravery, and stealth, and quick thinking –"

"And teamwork," Petra interrupted, not wanting to take all the credit for the dogs' escape from the thieves. She'd never have managed it on her own and all the dogs had contributed in some way, not to mention the wasp and his friends.

"Yes," agreed Lucy. "All of those things. But not looking pretty. That's not what people expect of you. So don't worry about posing for cameras if you don't like to do that. Just be Petra the Poltermeist."

ELEVEN

Christmas was approaching, but there was no time to get into the holiday mood as all the dogs continued to be busy. Lucy was still going out to schools on alternate days with staff from Peregrine Pets to deliver their Puppy Present assemblies. Petra had filmed her advertisement for the doggy energy drink, GO-GO DOG, and would soon attend a meeting, along with the Daleys, with the people making a computer game about her.

She was much more confident about it all since Lucy had spoken with her and told her it was okay to be herself, and this had been proven when she did the filming for the GO-GO DOG ad.

"I'm afraid she's not very good at sitting still and looking at the camera," Mr Daley had apologised as soon as he'd shaken everyone's hands on the day they met for the advert shoot. "She's quite shy."

"Ha! Not a problem, mate," the director laughed, a slight Australian accent lilting his words. "The product's an energy drink for dogs so, from what we know about her, she's perfect. That's why we booked her. There'll be no sitting around staring into cameras on this shoot."

They all bundled into a Land Rover and drove off to an area of countryside they were using as the set. This time Petra wasn't asked to look at the camera at all. In fact, she could forget there were cameras on her at all as she was filmed doing all the things she was best at, and now known for after her recent adventures: running up the side of a mountain, swimming in a lake, jumping over tree roots and stone walls, climbing gates and racing through fields. Petra loved every minute and the fact the director kept calling out, "yes mate", "cracking shot," and "perfect Petra," told her she was doing a good job and encouraged her. Lucy had been right. People liked her as she was.

At the end of the shoot, when Petra was panting and tired, they got their final shots of her sitting with her tongue hanging out, surrounded by bottles of GO-GO DOG.

"That's a wrap," the director called. "We'll edit it all together, and add the voice over. You should see it on the TV sometime in February. What a fantastic dog," he stroked Petra on the head. "She's just the perfect pooch to be associated with a product that gives long range energy. She never stops! She's awesome."

Petra was, in fact, pretty tired from her day's work, and slept all the way home in the car, but she'd enjoyed it and was now looking forward to her next engagement.

That just left Bella, who was still very popular in the school but had now progressed from being a reading buddy to appearing in the school play. Since some of the children had heard Mrs Daley use her nickname, Jingle Bella, and it was Christmas play season, they'd begged for her to be a part of it. As it happened, the play did have a part for a dog, which would have been performed by a child in costume, but it was quickly decided the part was Bella's. Someone would be given her lines to perform, but it was to be done as if she was the one speaking them.

It meant that Bella was now in school four days a week. She went in the late morning to do her reading work, then did an hour's play rehearsal in the afternoon. The Daleys might have worried it was too much for her, had it not been clear that she absolutely loved going to school and couldn't wait to get there. The school loved Bella too, and Mrs Cross said that attendance had gone up since Bella had begun her work in the library.

"Sometimes we even have to send them home," Mrs Cross told Mrs Daley one day. "We get them coming in even when they're unwell as they don't want to miss their Bella time."

Everything was going swimmingly with the Daleys managing the dogs' diaries perfectly so that they could all be in the right place at the right time until the video game people called to re-arrange their appointment.

"I'm afraid we can't do Monday," Mr Daley told them. "One of our other dogs is...er...working on Monday and we need to drop her off and pick her up."

But the video game people needed it to be on Monday, right away. They wanted the game out in time for Christmas, while Petra was popular and well known.

It would be a full day for Petra and the Daleys by the time they drove to the game maker's offices in Manchester, met with them, did some filming of Petra and drove back again. They wouldn't be able to drop Bella off at school and pick her up again later if they were going to be out all day. Lucy could go with them, as she had nothing on and was patient and sensible enough to sit still and wait while everything happened, but if they had to take Bella too, it would be a different matter. Bella was still a young dog who got bored easily. It would be better if she could stay in school all day, and be kept busy, but how could that work?

"Oh yes, of course, that'll be fine," Mrs Cross said when Mrs Daley explained the problem to her. "You can drop her off first thing during Breakfast Club. There'll be no shortage of volunteers to look after her, and I'll make sure they do this time," she added. "She can be in school as usual, but we'll give her some breaks so she can have some peace and quiet away from the kids, and have a nap if she needs one, since she'll be here all day. Then, after school on Mondays, there's Chess Club and Homework Club, so there'll be people in school until 5pm. If you're not back by then to pick her up, she can always come home with me and you can collect her from my house whenever you're heading home."

Mrs Daley thanked Mrs Cross for her kind offer and contacted the games people to confirm that they'd be able to make the meeting on Monday after all. Bella would go to school for the day and be surrounded by people keeping an eye on her. It was the perfect plan.

Or so it seemed.

TWELVE

As far as weekends in December went, it was a good one. The air was bitterly cold, and the Daleys wrapped up in warm coats with hats, gloves and scarves. It didn't stop them getting out for some bracing walks on the nearby forestry tracks, though.

The dogs all had coats they could wear too, but Lucy didn't like hers. She always dragged herself alongside walls or trees when wearing it to try and get rid of it. Petra didn't get to wear hers unless she was going to be on the lead the whole time, as she was constantly shredding them as she raced through the trees, snagging her coat on branches and brambles. The Daleys had given up putting coats on the two of them and because they didn't wear theirs, Bella didn't either and the three of them kept warm by keeping moving.

Their hot breath fogged the air as they crunched over the frost crisped grass with the fresh scent of the pine trees, making it feel even more like Christmas. It smelled like their house did at the moment, with the unusual addition of a brightly lit pine tree sitting in the corner of the living room.

As usual, Petra zinged through the trees, being the crazy pointer again as she searched for rabbits or deer to play with. Lucy and Bella stayed on the track with the Daleys drawing admiring glances and comments from everyone they passed on their walk.

Later, the dogs lay on the rug in front of the log fire listening to the snap, crackle and pop of the wood as it burned in the heat. They were so warm and snug, it made Lucy think of the wasp hibernating upstairs under the spare bed. She hoped he was sleeping soundly, ready to wake in the spring, when all the flowers started blooming again.

Lucy tried to stay awake and watch the news, but the soothing sounds of the fire were making it impossible. Her eyes were closing. The sounds around her dulled and slipped away as sleep wrapped itself around her.

"Lucy!" Her eyes snapped open as Bella suddenly barked her name. "Look!"

Lucy blinked rapidly to clear her vision and looked up at the TV screen. On it was a small red poodle with her three puppies, who were now nearly the same size as their mother.

"That's the poodle from the puppy farm," Petra said, her eyes locked on the screen.

The news reader confirmed her words. "I can now bring you news of Polly the poodle," she said. "Polly was recently recovered, along with her puppies, from a puppy farm being run by Jonas Moore and Patrick Adderly who will stand trial for theft and cruelty to animals in January. The men took Polly from her home over two years ago and her owners, Sally and James Wilson and their children, had given up hope of ever seeing her again. But we're pleased to tell you, the RSPCA has been able to trace Sally and James, who now live in Pontypool, Wales. Here they are being reunited with their long-lost pet."

The screen showed a family smothering the poodle and her pups with hugs and kisses. Their faces were a contradiction of joy and tears as they cuddled their missing dog.

"We're keeping all the puppies," the woman told the reporter, wiping her eyes on her sleeve. "This is our family and we'll never be separated again."

The news reader briefly reminded viewers about the stolen dogs escaping their captors and returning home, led by a pointer called Petra, before turning her attention to a story about a car manufacturer.

Petra sighed happily. She hoped the boxer, the cocker spaniel and the border terrier had also been reunited with their humans, or found nice new humans who would give them the lives they deserved.

"You did that," Lucy said to Petra. "All those dogs are safe and happy thanks to you, including our Bella here."

The three of them snuggled close together and drifted off into a contented sleep. As she closed her eyes and felt the warm, solid presence of Lucy and Petra beside her, Bella wondered what would have happened to her if Petra hadn't come to save her. *I'd probably still be stuck in the puppy farm,* she thought, remembering her old life and how the humans she'd met had been nothing like the Daleys. Those people couldn't be bothered with her and showed her no love or attention. She was so lucky to have met Petra and come to live with her and Lucy and the Daleys. Now

Christmas was coming. Her first Christmas. She couldn't have been happier.

THIRTEEN

On Monday morning, Bella couldn't wait to get to school. Mr and Mrs Daley dropped her off at 8.15 a.m. before continuing on the drive to Manchester to meet the video game producers. Bella was pleased that she wasn't going with them. It would be boring just hanging around all day while the humans talked about Petra. She'd have a far more interesting day at school.

"See you later, Ding Dong," said Mr Daley from the front seat of the car, as Mrs Daley walked her to the school gates to hand her over to a waiting teacher.

"Be good, Jingles." Mrs Daley gave her a quick pat before leaving her with the teacher and hurrying back to the warmth of the car.

Bella was a real part of the family now as, like Lucy and Petra, she hardly ever got called by her real name. Both the Daleys used a variety of nicknames whenever they spoke to her. Clever Bella knew all of her extra names.

Breakfast club was amazing. Bella had already eaten before she left the house that morning, but she couldn't turn down the hot buttered toast being offered to her by the children. She took care not to snatch it from them like Lucy would have; her chops making a *nom* sound as they quickly devoured anything she was offered. Bella always liked to smell and assess food before taking it gently. The Daleys often laughed at her suspicion and remarked that Bella must think they were trying to poison her.

The children loved the way she delicately accepted their toast crusts and giggled when they were told off for giving them to her. Bella wagged her tail, enjoying all the attention.

Library duty followed breakfast. First, it was a group of older children. Bella knew them all by sight and smell and greeted them in her usual enthusiastic manner, 'Bella bombing' them when they entered the library. Once she'd nibbled everyone's ears, she was happy to flop down amongst the bean bags with them and listen to them reading. Bella loved stories. Today it was a story about a girl trapped in a frozen world. She needed to find a way out to get back home, but she was slowly freezing. If she couldn't escape soon, she'd turn to ice and remain there forever. Bella was disappointed when the bell rang for play time before they'd finished the story. She wanted to know what happened in the end.

The day progressed with play time in the yard, then more reading with a different group. A little boy called Freddie squeaked with delight as he raced into the library to see the reading dog. Bella sensed a desperation from the child. The way he was always so overjoyed to see her and the way he constantly stroked her told her he needed a friend. Bella knew how that felt and sat with the boy throughout the session. Other children called her to them and she quickly greeted everyone before returning to him. She didn't want to leave anyone out, but she knew Freddie needed her more than the others.

After that she had a break for a nap, followed by lunchtime in the staff room. Bella wasn't allowed into the hall with the children at lunchtime in case all two hundred of them tried to share their food with her, but the teachers couldn't resist giving her a selection of titbits from their dinners either so she still got some treats.

When lunch was over, it was time for Christmas play rehearsals. The older children had their own separate performance, and they practised first. Bella was a part of the younger children's play and they had their time in the hall for the last hour of the day.

It was chaos! Some children had parts and lines to perform from memory, some were narrators and had to read out loud at the correct part of the performance. Others had non-speaking roles, and some were musicians who couldn't stop rattling, shaking and blowing into their instruments until one teacher made the children put them down and said they weren't allowed to touch them until she gave a signal that they were to do so.

"I can't hear myself think!" she said, her eyes widening in her reddening face.

Then there was Bella, the only non-human performer in the play. As she couldn't speak, one of the children was to be her voice and say her lines. Freddie's teacher had noticed his special attachment to Bella and chose him to be her stage partner.

The pair sat together in the hall, waiting for their turn. Freddie's legs jiggled, and he drummed his fingernails against the hardwood floor. Bella thought his restlessness was excitement about the play, so it surprised her when he suddenly jumped up and hurried out of the hall. All the teachers and children were distracted so no-one noticed him leave.

Something wasn't right. Bella just knew it. She stood up and followed Freddie's scent. It didn't lead to the bathroom, as she'd expected. It led into reception ... and out of the front door, which was held open on a catch. A chill wind blew in and Bella shivered. She wondered why Freddie had gone outside as she knew this was against the rules. There were no adults around to see what had happened so it was up to her. She had to bring him back inside.

Bella went through the door, onto the path outside, expecting to see Freddie there. There was no sign of him. He'd gone.

The young dog quivered with indecision. She didn't want to leave the school. She might get lost ... or stolen again. She wanted to stay safe with the Daleys, and she didn't want to worry them after what they'd suffered with Lucy and Petra both going missing in the past. It was too big a risk to go after Freddie, but he was outside, alone in the cold. She knew what that was like. She barked, hoping Freddie would hear her and turn back. A cloud of condensation formed in the air as her voice echoed around her and she strained her eyes and ears, hoping to see the little boy. There was nothing.

If I go after him, I might never find my way back to the Daleys. I could end up all alone again, she thought. But I need to be brave, like Lucy and Petra. I don't know what he's doing, but he shouldn't be alone. He could be in danger. He's my friend, and he needs my help.

All her instincts told her to think of herself and go back inside, but she ignored them. Putting her nose to the ground, she picked up the boy's scent. It was so familiar to her, but for the first time, she realised what is was; the smell of sadness.

Taking one last look at the school behind her, Bella made her decision. She chose Freddie.

FOURTEEN

Petra's meeting in Manchester had gone well. So well, they'd over run and were late setting off to head home.

Like the dog food company who'd seen Petra on the news and decided she'd be a good representative for their canine energy drink, since she appeared to be leading the pack of stolen dogs, the video game producers had thought the same thing. With Petra being seen all over the place on TV and in magazines, it was perfect timing to bring out a Petra based game while she was hot property.

After talking to the Daleys and meeting Petra in person (so to speak), the producers decided the to call the game The Crazy Pointer after Petra excitedly presented them all with their own door mat. She bundled it up in her mouth, like a package, and thrust it into the face of each of the producers, wiggling her whole body madly as they tried to stroke her. After Lucy's pep talk, Petra was much happier about being herself and her good cheer was clear to see.

"She's like a shark," Mr Daley joked. "She can't stay still – always moving!"

The producers loved this and filmed Petra in a variety of situations that would later be animated. They decided the game would have a number of levels of increasing difficulty and craziness that would link to Petra's personality and her recent rescue adventures. Given Petra's love of hunting, the first level involved trying to find as many rabbits, hares, pheasants and deer as possible as they flashed up briefly on screen in crazy hiding places. Players earned pointer points for every one Petra touched.

After that, level 2 linked to Petra's athleticism. Players had to guide her up and down mountain passes, through forests and lakes, across roads and over walls and fences without leading her into any of the hazards that popped up along the way.

Level 3 progressed to Petra the rescue dog and players were given a variety of situations, from dogs trapped inside burning buildings, or stranded on an island with a flooded river rising around it, or stuck on a narrow mountain ledge, to deal with in role as Petra.

Finally, level 4, the most difficult level, involved Petra's gift of invisibility and moving around like a ghost. In the final level, the game recreated the true story of the stolen dogs that Petra was known for. Players had to help Petra and the other dogs travel home, making use of unorthodox hiding places to avoid being caught by the thieves who were following them. The dogs might hide up a tree, jump on a bus or take cover in a crocodile enclosure at the zoo.

They filmed Petra leaping on and off boxes of different heights, through hoops and tunnels, climbing over gates and carrying various objects in her mouth against a green screen behind her. She was so absorbed in the physical activity, she completely forgot she was being filmed. It was just like playtime, and she loved every minute. Lucy watched her in action with pride in her eyes, pleased that Petra's true personality was being captured.

The only thing left to do was complete the animation and decide on a theme tune for the game.

"We'll have to discuss that another time," said Mrs Daley. "We have to pick our other dog up from school."

The producers raised their eyebrows and looked at each other, clearly thinking, *who sends their dog to school?* But Mrs Daley didn't notice. She was in too much of a hurry to leave. It was already nearly 4 p.m.

Once they were all back in the car and preparing to drive home, Mrs Daley pulled her phone out of her bag and found the number she wanted.

"I'm so sorry," she began as soon as the phone was answered. "We've been longer than we expected. We're only just setting off from Manchester now, so we won't make it back in time to collect Bella from school by 5 p.m. If you're still happy to take her to your house, that would be perfect. We'll come and get her from you, but you may want to keep her in the kitchen. She's used to getting on our sofa, you see, and I wouldn't want her jumping up on your -"

The voice on the other end interrupted Mrs Daley, and she listened, not believing what she was hearing.

"What do you mean, she's *gone missing*?"

Mr Daley frowned and stopped reversing the car out of its parking space, blocking the road as he looked to his wife for explanation. Someone honked their horn at him, so he pulled back in.

"Have you checked everywhere? Last time we thought they'd gone missing, they were there all along."

Mrs Daley listened to the reply for a minute, then said, "We'll be as quick as we can," before ending the call.

"What is it about our dogs?" she cried to her husband. "All the Daley's dogs like to disappear!"

"What's happened?" Mr Daley asked gently, hoping to calm his wife's panic.

"It's Bella. She's gone missing from school. A little boy too. There's a search party out looking for them. It's dark!"

Mr Daley's heart dropped into his socks, but he said, "I'm sure they'll be fine. Let's get home."

Hoping his words were true, Mr Daley pulled out and began a nerve-wracking drive home.

FIFTEEN

When the Daleys pulled up outside the school at around half-past six, all the lights were on and police cars were parked outside, their blue lights pulsing in the darkness. Mr and Mrs Daley parked up and promised Lucy and Petra they wouldn't be long.

"Hopefully, Bella and the little boy will have been found by now," Mrs Daley said, even though she'd had no call from Mrs Cross to tell her this, "and we can all go home together. Poor Lu and Meist have been cooped up in the car for hours. They need their tea. We won't be long girls," she said to the two dogs in the boot of the car, before throwing herself out and running to the school's front door, huddled against the sleet. Mr Daley followed. There was no way he could just sit in the car and wait. He had to know what was going on.

Inside, the staff room was packed. Several of the teachers were still there, some police officers, and Mrs Cross who was sitting with a tearful man and an angry looking woman.

"- probably mauling our son to death, that dog is. I've heard Dalmatians can be aggressive, and you've brought one into the school that's not properly trained or anything," the woman said.

"Mrs Fisher, you know Freddie loves Bella. He's benefited most from her being here. His reading has improved so much since he's been working with her. Yes, she's young and energetic, but she's completely friendly with the children. She's never shown any aggression. Freddie left the school on his own so we don't know if Bella is with him or not." As Mrs Cross reached out to place a hand on the woman's arm, she noticed the Daleys standing in the doorway and jumped up to greet them.

"Mrs Daley, Mr Daley, I'm so sorry about this. I -"

"What you apologising to them for?" the angry woman spat. "It's just a dog they've lost. What about my son?" Before Mrs Cross could respond, the woman's husband put an arm around her and pulled her into him, shushing her like a child.

Mrs Cross indicated the Daleys should follow her into her office where they could speak in private.

"I'm afraid that Freddie and Bella have been missing for several hours now," she said, leaning heavily against her desk. Her face was ashen and her usually bright, twinkling eyes were stone. "Mr Green, the Year 1 teacher noticed they weren't in the hall at around three this afternoon. We searched the school and the grounds, but there was no sign of them, so we looked at the CCTV." Mrs Cross gulped and scrunched her eyes closed for a second before she continued.

"This afternoon, we had a delivery from the caterers. They normally deliver straight into the kitchen, but the entrance outside the doors was icy and hadn't been gritted so it was too dangerous. They had to come through the main entrance instead. Normally, the gates and main doors are locked and only Mrs Lowther, the receptionist, can open them. But this afternoon, the door was held open on the catch so the deliveries could be brought inside. The CCTV shows that Mrs Lowther had to leave her position to escort the delivery men to the kitchen, to show them the way. And while she's away...that's when we see little Freddie slip out of the door." She bit back a sob. "He didn't have a coat on or anything and look at this weather!" She pointed to the black windows distorted by the sleet that was sliding down the panes. "He's out in this and has been for hours! No-one has any idea where he could be. All the expected places have been checked but there's no sign of him."

Mrs Cross's face contorted as she battled to keep control of her emotions. Mrs Daley didn't like to upset her further, but she needed to know about Bella.

"What about Bella?" she asked, followed by, "It looks like the police are out looking for them?"

"Yes, along with half the neighbourhood and the teaching staff. We're still waiting for police search dogs to arrive though - the local ones were already 'on a job' so they're sending some from Penrith. They've said that dogs will struggle to find them in this weather though...rain washes the scent away..." Mrs Cross stopped speaking and stared into the black window, seeing nothing but her own distorted misery reflected back at her.

"Er...Bella?" Mr Daley reminded her gently.

"Oh yes, Bella. The CCTV picks up Bella a couple of minutes after Freddie, and just seconds before Mrs Lowther returns to the desk. She's got her nose down, sniffing the carpet. When the police watched it, they thought she was following his scent. She knows him well, after all. It appears she's gone after him. We're hoping they'll be found together. There's nothing you can do here. It's best if you go home with your other dogs and wait there. I'll call you the minute we hear anything. Hopefully it won't be long. I'd better get back." She indicated that she needed to return to the staff room where she'd left Freddie's parents.

"Yes, of course," Mrs Daley agreed as the headteacher showed them out and headed back to the staff room.

When the Daleys stepped back outside, they immediately noticed that the sleet had given way to snow. Big, fat snowflakes fell serenely from the sky. Normally it would have been a beautiful sight, but both of the Daleys were thinking the same thing: a little boy and their Bella were outside somewhere in the dark, no doubt wet from all the sleet, and now it was snowing. If someone didn't find them soon, they'd freeze. Where could they be that they hadn't been found already, when search teams had been out for hours, looking for them without success?

Their attention was diverted away from the swirling snow by the sight of their car rocking at the bottom of the path. Lucy and Petra were inside, both frantically scrabbling at the boot door, desperate to get out.

"Oh dear, they must be desperate for the toilet," Mr Daley said. "They've been in the car for hours. We'd better let them out for a quick wee in case they can't wait 'til we get home."

He opened the car and grabbed the dogs' leads off the back seat. Mrs Daley lifted the door of the boot, saying 'wait' to the dogs as she always did. They were well trained to always wait until their leads were clipped on before they were allowed to jump out of the car. They always waited. They were good dogs. But not that night. Before the door was even half way up, both dogs leapt from the car, nearly knocking Mrs Daley over, and sped away into the darkness.

"NOOOO!" Mrs Daley's wail followed them as they disappeared.

SIXTEEN

Lucy and Petra knew it was bad news when the Daleys emerged from the school without Bella. She hadn't been found, and she'd been out in the cold for hours. Bella couldn't be lost; she could follow her own scent back to the school if she wanted to return, unless the rain had washed it away. That meant she was either stranded somewhere and didn't know how to find her way back, or she was staying out on purpose. It must be something to do with the child who'd also gone missing. Either way, she needed their help. They both knew from experience that humans were no good on search and rescue missions; their sense of smell and eyesight were poor at the best of times, but in the dark, they'd be completely useless. They would have to find Bella.

When Mrs Daley opened the boot of the car, thinking the dogs just needed out to relieve themselves, they both did what they'd never done before: they ignored her command and streaked out past her like a pair of racing greyhounds. Before the Daleys could grab either of them by the collar, Petra picked up Bella's faint scent. It was barely there, but Petra spent her life with Bella snuggled up right under her nose, so she breathed in the young dog's smell, even in her sleep. Bella had her own bed, but often squeezed in beside the pointer.

"This way." Petra gave a short, sharp bark to Lucy, and the pair disappeared together down the street.

They were soon away from the Daleys and heading out of the town. Petra was so focussed on trying to stay on Bella's scent she didn't even notice some pigeons that she would normally have chased, or the spilled chips that she would have eaten. Neither did she notice cars travelling up and down the road. Lucy had to be her eyes.

"Car!" she barked several times, grabbing Petra's collar in her teeth to stop the concentrating dog from stepping right into the path of oncoming vehicles.

Soon they crossed a railway track, with Lucy warning Petra to look out for trains, and followed a coastal path with sand dunes on their left. The smell of the sea was strong and threatened to overpower Bella's fading trail.

"Why would she have come this way?" wondered Lucy. "Is she heading to the beach?" Lucy hoped not. Despite the darkness, she could see that the tide was almost fully in. The waves were gobbling their way up to the dunes. If Bella had gone onto the beach, the creeping tide could have come in around her and cut her off, blocking her way back to the path. Lucy couldn't bear to think about it.

"No, I don't think so," Petra said, inhaling deeply at the railway sleepers. "I think she's crossed back over. Let's go down here."

They crossed the track again and headed into a tunnel that went under the road. It was like being swallowed by a humongous whale. A flood of human smells engulfed their nostrils and made it impossible to pick up anything of Bella. Petra recognised beer bottles, cigarette smoke, pizza, salt and vinegar crisps and body spray from the horde of scents that lurked in the tunnel. Hackles rose along her back as she crept through in the pitch blackness, taking care not to step on any shards of glass that might have littered the floor.

"Where now?" asked Lucy as they eventually left the tunnel and came out at the side of a road. Cars were still whizzing past; snowflakes being batted aside by windscreen wipers.

"I don't know," replied Petra. The smells from the tunnel still filled her nostrils, with the sharp chemical scent of fuel from the cars joining in. "I can't smell her anymore."

Lucy watched helplessly as Petra sniffed all around her, trying to find Bella's scent. She couldn't. "It's gone," Petra said.

Lucy couldn't accept that and she joined in sniffing urgently all around her. Her nose wasn't as sensitive as Petra's, but she was determined to find something.

Both dogs tried their hardest to find the tiniest scrap of a scent that could at least tell them which direction to head in, but there was nothing.

Lucy raised her head and felt the snow on her face. It had thickened and was starting to lay on the ground, blanketing everything in white. Her eyes met Petra's, and she knew they were both thinking the same thing. Wherever Bella's scent might have been, they'd lost it; it was now buried beneath the snow. If they were going to find Bella now, they'd need another way. But what?

SEVENTEEN

"What now? Should we split up to search separately or stay together?" Petra asked Lucy. She may have recently rescued nine other dogs from captivity and led them to safety, but she hadn't done it alone. The other dogs had all played their part in some way to help her and each other. Petra was pleased to have Lucy with her this time to share the decision making with. She'd found it scary to have to think for herself whilst in a position of huge responsibility. She was good at action, not thinking things through.

"We stick together," said Lucy, her soft brown eyes dark with determination. "We don't want one of us to get lost too."

Petra let out the breath she'd been holding. She'd been hoping Lucy would say that. She felt braver with her friend by her side. They were a team.

"Which way should we go?" she asked, trusting Lucy to know what to do.

Lucy looked to her left and right, then she looked straight across to the other side of the road. "We need to think like a human," she said. "Like a human child. Bella will be following the little boy, so wherever he is, that's where we'll find her. I don't think he'd have tried to cross this road. Not here anyway. It's too busy. And I don't think he'd have turned right, as that's going back the way we've just come. He must've left the school to go somewhere, so I think we should turn left and keep heading north."

Petra marvelled at Lucy's clever thinking and tried to add to it, wanting to show her friend that she could help to reason this out.

"Look, up the road there," she said, "there's some traffic lights. Humans use them to cross the road. The green man comes on and tells the cars to stop, then the humans go across. Maybe the little boy used the green man?"

"Good thinking," said Lucy. "Let's go."

The two dogs trotted up the pavement towards the traffic lights and waited for the green man to stop the cars. But nothing happened. The cars continued to zoom by and the dogs shivered.

"Where's the green man?" asked Petra through chattering teeth.

Lucy looked up at the pole the lights were mounted on to see if there was a handle or something to push. She spotted a small white button on a black box mounted onto the pole. The box said 'Wait'. Just like she did at home, where she jumped up and leaned on door handles to open the door, she stood up and placed a paw over the white button. A few seconds later, the box said 'Walk' and the green man appeared.

"There he is!" Petra said.

"The cars have stopped. Let's go," said Lucy,

stepping out onto the road. The drivers at the front of

the queuing traffic couldn't believe their eyes: two dogs

without humans using a pelican crossing to get across the road wasn't a sight they were used to.

Once they reached the opposite side, the dogs turned left again and continued up the pavement. A row of terraced houses stretched up the street. Lights poured out of windows onto the dark street and Christmas trees twinkled invitingly. Lucy and Petra looked at the people inside who were warm and cosy and safe and felt their stomachs rumble. The heavy snow made them cold and wet. They'd have loved to go inside one of the houses and get warm by the fire, but while Bella and the little boy were out in this weather, they couldn't stop until they found them. Doubt nibbled away at them, though. Would they find them? With no scent to follow, they had no idea where to go. They could be heading in completely the wrong direction. The poor Daleys had all three of their dogs missing and Lucy could imagine just how worried they would be. She hoped it would all be worth it in the end and that, by the end of the evening, they would all be back together in their own home in front of the fire with full bellies.

That idea seemed a long way off, though.

The row of terraced houses came to an end and there was a steep grassy embankment with trees at the bottom. The dogs stopped again to decide where to go now. There was still no scent to be detected from the snowy pavement, but it seemed like it was the most likely route to follow. Why would a little boy go down a steep slope into trees? There'd be no reason for that, so the two of them continued on.

Until something caught Lucy's eye.

"Petra, look at that," she said to stop her friend, who was focussed on following the pavement. "What is it?"

It was a scrap of blue fabric caught on a jagged edge of a lamp post. It looked like a car had collided with it recently as some yellow tape fluttered from it, showing it hadn't been fixed. It was slightly bent and twisted about a third of the way up, with a small piece of metal protruding out towards the grass.

Petra quickly sniffed the fabric. It smelled of baked beans and glue and washing powder and...boy. "It's him!" she said. "They've been this way, and he's caught his school jumper here and ripped it." Petra tensed and pricked her ears, straining to hear any small sound that would provide a clue. She closed her eyes and listened harder, her nose twitching as she sniffed the air, hoping to pick up more of the boy's scent. All she could smell was cold. It burned her nostrils as she inhaled it.

Lucy decided to try something.

"Bella?" she barked towards the trees at the bottom of the embankment.

Nothing.

"Bella?" she barked again, louder.

Petra turned her head and trotted a few paces further up the path. Then she stopped and lifted a front paw, pointing down the bank. "Did you hear that?" she asked Lucy.

"What?" asked Lucy. "I didn't hear anything."

"I'm sure I heard something," said Petra, still pointing. "From down there."

Lucy's almost frozen heart boomed inside her as a spark of hope flared.

"Come on then, let's go."

Without wasting another second, the two of them bounded down the bank towards the cluster of trees waiting at the bottom.

EIGHTEEN

"Bella! Bella!" they barked. Petra dashed through the trees, searching, but Lucy stood still, listening. It was dark in the woods apart from the white ground. The canopy of trees were bare of leaves and their boughs were heavy with snow. Lucy had no idea how Petra could move so fast among the trees in the limited light without crashing into anything. She seemed to have super senses and moved like a ghost, touching nothing.

"Here, here, here!" Petra yipped excitedly. She'd got a strong scent of boy from a tree stump. "They've been here. They can't be far away."

"Listen," said Lucy. "I heard something."

Petra stilled and pricked up her ears, looking around her as if she was trying to tune in to the sound. "I heard it," she said suddenly. "This way."

Petra hurried off to the left, with Lucy following. "Bella!" she barked. "Where are you?"

There was no answer, and no sign of a spotty dog or a child. The only thing they could see was a lumpy sheet of plastic a little way off. Petra went to sniff it.

"OWowowowow!" Petra ululated as the strong scent of her quarry filled her nostrils and made her brain cells pop with excitement. This was just what it was like when she got the scent of a rabbit or a deer. It took her over and made her have to chase it. But this quarry wasn't running away. It was lying still under the plastic.

Petra tunnelled under the sheet as Lucy joined her and shoved herself under too. Lying underneath were Bella and the little boy. Bella's eyes were open, but they were flat and lifeless. The boy's eyes were closed and his face looked blue. Lucy frowned. They'd seen a piece of his blue school jumper caught on a lamp post, but he was wearing a huge black coat. How could he have caught his jumper if he had that on? He also wore a pair of gloves. Except they weren't a pair. One was a child's, rainbow striped and multi-coloured, while the other looked like a man's work glove. It was far too big for the boy's right hand and would have looked comical if the situation had been less serious.

"No, no, no!" Petra panicked. Lucy put her ear to the boy's chest, then to Bella's.

"They're both still alive. Just. I can hear their heartbeats, but they're weak and they're barely breathing. We have to get help, right now!"

Petra was poised and ready to race. "I'll run back to the houses we passed. You come up to the top of the embankment and wait. As soon as you see someone, bark and get them to follow you. If people are out looking for Bella and the boy, they'll probably think that you're Bella and follow you. Let's go."

Reluctantly, Lucy followed Petra out of the trees and back up the bank to the pavement. She didn't want to leave Bella and the little boy, but she knew Petra was right. They needed to get help immediately, before it was too late. She didn't say so to Petra, but she knew they didn't have long.

Petra ran like a bullet back down to the row of terraced houses and barked like Lucy had never heard her before. It was frantic and full of urgency. She jumped up and scratched at the window of one house before dashing off to the next house and doing the same thing there. She went down the whole row, repeating the action. Soon, doors were opening and people were sticking their heads out to see what was going on. They had their arms folded across chests and didn't want to come outside into the snow.

"Go away, you daft dog," one old man in slippers said. "Where's your owner? Go home." He slammed his door.

"No! Help, help, help!" Petra barked madly, spinning in circles. Lucy, way up the road, could work out what was happening and started barking too.

"There's a dog out on the street behaving very strangely," one woman said into her mobile phone. "It's like it wants us to come outside for some reason." She stepped out and looked up the road to where Lucy could be seen in the distance. "Yes, actually there is a Dalmatian further up the road. It's barking its head off too." She listened to the voice on the other end and her eyes widened. Suddenly, she became very animated. "Hey," she said to her neighbour, who was about to go back inside and close the door. "Get your coat on and knock on everyone's door. There's a kid gone missing from St Patrick's school and he's believed to be with a Dalmatian dog. There's one up the road making a big fuss. And look at this one – they're trying to tell us something. Get everyone up there. I'm calling the police and an ambulance. The wee lad has been out in this weather for hours. Hurry!"

Petra spun in circles, wagging her tail like a whisk. *Yes, it was working!* People were coming out of their houses wearing hats and coats and wellington

145

boots and were running up the road to where Lucy was waiting for them.

"Quick, this way! Follow me," she barked. The humans could only hear 'woof, woof, woof, woof', of course, but they understood what she meant. Some of them disappeared down the bank in pursuit of Lucy, while others remained on the pavement, waiting to direct the police when they arrived.

In just a matter of minutes, the dark was lit up with flashing blue lights and the sound of sirens slicing through the snow as police cars and an ambulance screeched to a halt beside the waiting people. Police and paramedics flung themselves out of their vehicles and charged down the bank and into the trees.

Petra stood on the pavement and watched. *We've done it*, she thought. *We've found them. But are we in time?* Lucy hadn't mentioned the seriousness of the situation to her, but she knew. She just hoped they weren't too late.

NINETEEN

It was Christmas Eve when Bella returned home after several days at the vets. On the night of the rescue, the little boy was whisked away in an ambulance. Police officers had wrapped Bella in a swathe of blankets and bundled her into the car along with Lucy and Petra. Lucy had immediately started licking Bella's face, but the young dog barely stirred. Her face was like a block of ice.

The police knew who Lucy and Petra were, since both of them were local celebrities now, and also knew of their connection to Robbins' Veterinary Practice. They raced straight there, sirens blaring and laser-beam blue lights flashing, to be met by Wren Robbins who'd been called to alert her of the emergency. By the time the Daleys found out what was going on, and arrived at the surgery, Bella was being treated for hypothermia.

"She's been out for hours in freezing temperatures," the vet explained. "I'm surprised she's still alive, to be honest. Her body temperature has dropped so low, I need to treat her and monitor her for a few days. There could be complications, I'm afraid."

"Complications? Like what?" Mrs Daley said, grey bags of weariness pulling at the skin under her eyes.

"I'm sure she'll be fine, don't worry," the vet said, not wanting to give the poor woman any further stress. "She's wrapped up, and on heating pads. I'm checking her temperature every ten minutes, plus her heart and lungs. I may need to heat her internally using fluids, but she's young and strong. She has every chance of making a full recovery."

The Daleys left Bella in the vet's care and took Lucy and Petra home, as they were also cold and hungry. It had been nice to see Gomez and Gizmo, the vet's dogs briefly at the surgery, and it was a relief to know that Bella was in the best place, but they were still worried about her.

The Daleys made an extra big fuss of them that night. They both had a lovely tea and a nice bath, then they lay in front of the fire, wrapped in towels as the Daleys discussed the day.

"This could have been another episode for The Crazy Pointer game," Mr Daley said as he leaned back wearily on the sofa.

"Yes," Mrs Daley agreed. "Today, all three of our dogs went missing. It's getting to be a regular thing. I'm sure that Lucy and Petra took off because they wanted to find Bella, and thank goodness they did, since the police dogs, when they eventually arrived, couldn't pick up the smell. The search party was looking in the wrong direction too. No-one has any idea why the little boy was found where he was."

"It was just as well Bella was with him. She probably saved his life." Mr Daley recalled the conversation they'd had with a police officer at the vet's surgery. He'd told them the child had been found wearing an assortment of random clothes that didn't belong to him, plus he was protected from the weather by a large sheet of plastic he'd pulled over himself. He was cuddled up to the Dalmatian and her body heat would have helped to keep him warm. Plus, there was no doubt that they'd been found because Lucy and Petra had detected the faint scent of their friend.

"We're going to have to set up Daley's Dog Rescues," Mrs Daley said, "since our dogs are always going to the rescue." She was joking, as she didn't really think Bella had done much rescuing, apart from keeping the missing boy warm, but when Bella returned home days later, Lucy and Petra learned that she'd done much more.

Bella was quieter than usual when the Daleys brought her home on Christmas Eve. The vet had explained that the ordeal had taken a lot out of her and she still needed rest and to be kept warm. Petra made room for her when the young dog came into her bed to snuggle up, like she had done when she'd first arrived. Once settled in, Bella told her story.

"I thought Freddie maybe needed the toilet when he got up and left me in the hall, but there was something about him...something not right. I thought I'd better go after him," she began. "His scent didn't lead to the bathroom, though. It headed towards reception, so I followed it and saw the front doors were open. They aren't usually. The boy's smell went right through the doors so I followed. I thought he'd be outside on the front grass, but he wasn't. His scent went right down the path, onto the pavement and across the road. I knew something was wrong then. Small humans aren't meant to be out on the roads on their own. It felt bad and it was cold. He's my friend though, and I knew I had to find him and get him back to school safely, so I went after him."

Bella went on with her story, explaining how it soon started to sleet and, without her coat, she was all wet in no time. She had sped up and caught up to the little boy. She'd tried to round him up and steer him back to school, but he wouldn't go. He just kept saying, *'I'm sure he lives near the trains.'* Bella didn't know what that meant, or where he was trying to get to, so she kept trying, without success, to get him to turn around.

After they'd passed a row of terraced houses and were walking alongside a grass embankment, the boy had stopped and looked down the bank. "I think it's down there," he'd said to Bella. "On the other side of

those trees is a football field and Jack lives near there."
Fearing he would slip if he tried to head down the bank,
Bella tried to block him with her body. Her helpful plan
backfired, though, when he tripped over her and
caught his jumper on a twisted lamp post. It ripped
and left a hole in his jumper.

"We found it!" Petra interjected excitedly. "Then I
got his scent. That's how I found you. Your scent on
the ground had been washed away." Nodding
thoughtfully, Bella continued explaining. Falling over
her and catching himself on the lamp post made
Freddie lose his balance. He stumbled and tripped onto
the wet grass and rolled all the way to the bottom of
the slope.

Freddie was crying when Bella reached him. He'd
hurt his foot and was clutching it in his hands. After a
few minutes, he tried to crawl and headed into the
woods, possibly looking for somewhere to shelter. The

sleet had turned into snow by this time and it was almost dark. But he hadn't been able to move very far and stopped.

"He just sat and cried," Bella said, "calling for his mum. I didn't know what to do; I didn't know where his mum was. I thought maybe I should go and look for help, but I didn't want to leave him alone in the dark. And I knew from the story that we were in danger. We could freeze to death."

"What story?" Lucy asked.

"The one I'd heard earlier in the day about the girl who was trapped in the frozen world," Bella explained. "If she didn't get out in time, she'd freeze and stay there forever. So, I knew I had to keep us warm. I sniffed around in the trees and found a jacket. It was covered in leaves and wasn't very clean. It was soggy on the outside too, but it had to do so I took that to him and he put it on. On my next trip, I found two gloves. One was on the ground; another had been placed on the end of a low branch. They were different colours and sizes, but it didn't matter. I felt a bit better for Freddie, but it was still snowing and there was nothing for me. I had one last look around and found a piece of plastic sticking out from under the snow. I pulled at it and it was a big sheet, so I took it back to Freddie and dragged it over him. Then I got under and pressed myself up next to him to keep us both warm."

She paused as she remembered it all. She didn't look like the confident, playful, happy pup Lucy and Petra were used to.

"It was so dark," she whispered. "And cold. I couldn't move. I couldn't feel my body. I was sure we were going to freeze...but then I heard you calling my name." She looked at Lucy and Petra. "I thought I was dreaming. How could you two be there looking for me? I didn't believe it. But I kept hearing you. I tried to call back, but I could barely make a sound. I was so weak. I didn't think you'd be able to hear me."

"Well, we did. Just," said Lucy. And now, here we all are, together. We've had some exciting and dangerous adventures this year, but they're all in the past now. From now on, we're going to keep our noses out of trouble and lead normal, quiet lives like other dogs."

"Sounds good to me," Bella replied.

TWENTY

The dogs were woken the next morning by Mr Daley's spirited singing of Jingle Bells as he came down the stairs and opened the door into the kitchen.

"Jingle all the way! Merry Christmas girls," he bent down and gave them all a kiss and a belly rub as they lay, blinking and drowsy in their warm beds. Once belly rubs were over and the dogs were awake, Mr Daley put their coats on, clipped them all onto their leads and took them for a quick walk while Mrs Daley started making breakfasts.

"Happy Christmas!" All the dog walkers greeted each other merrily as they passed on the streets. Most people were inside, still in their pyjamas opening presents, but all those with dogs had to wait for present opening until walkies were complete. They didn't mind. It was a cold, crisp morning, but weak rays of sun were pushing through the clouds. Frost lining the grass and bare branches on trees glistened as the light caught them. It was a pretty sight, but it reminded Bella of her recent ordeal and she shrank into her fleecy jacket, welcoming its warmth.

Soon they came back to the house and were greeted with the smell of turkey cooking in the oven. The dogs' bowls were full of their own special dog food, but they weren't interested in that for now. Mrs Daley was buttering thick, crusty white toasted bread. All the dogs loved toast, and their nostrils quivered. They sat down to beg, ignoring their own food, and sure enough, the Daleys shared their breakfast with them, as they always did. Once there was nothing left on plates but crumbs, the dogs turned their attention to the food in their bowls.

"Greedy girls," Mrs Daley chuckled. "Not one breakfast, but two!"

Presents came next. The whole family moved into the living room and sat around the Christmas tree. The dogs got their stockings first. Each of them received some tasty treats, and Petra and Bella received a new toy each. Bella's crocodile squeaked, much to her delight, and she spent the rest of the morning squeaking it in her mouth, or batting it with her paw. Lucy wasn't interested in house toys, so she got a new ball to take on walks to play with.

Then it was time for their main present: a tracking collar each.

"If only I'd got around to ordering these sooner," Mr Daley said as he fastened Bella's blue collar around her neck. "We'd have known exactly where you were when you went missing, wouldn't we? We could have had you found straight away."

Next, Petra received hers: a bright orange one to complement her brown markings, and then Lucy: plain black for her to match her spots. Bella's collar was blue to link to her full, registered name: Lady Bluebell.

"There'll be no more going missing now," Mr Daley stood back to admire the dogs in their collars and consult the app on his phone that linked to the collars. "I can always find you with this." He looked at the screen to confirm that the map displayed their location accurately.

"Yes, better late than never," Mrs Daley agreed, looking at the screen too. "Now it's time for our prezzies."

The day was glorious. After a huge Christmas dinner of turkey, potatoes, pigs in blankets, a medley of vegetables and delicious gravy, which was, of course, shared with the dogs, it was time for another walk. This time they went to some open fields where the dogs could run free and sniff to their heart's content. Lucy chased her ball, doing forward rolls every time she dropped her head to snatch it off the ground. At one point, Petra did a disappearing act, as usual, but instead of worrying where she might be, Mr Daley just whipped out his phone and consulted the dot that was Petra. He sighed happily, seeing that she was nearby, probably looking for rabbits in the grass verge over the hill.

While they were walking home, Mrs Daley's phone rang. "Who could that be, calling on Christmas Day?" she wondered aloud. "We've already spoken to the relatives." She drew it out of her pocket, fumbling with her gloves so that she almost dropped it. "It's Mrs Cross," she said, as she answered it. "Hello?"

There were lots of 'mm hmms' and 'really?' and 'gosh' before she finished off with, "thanks for letting us know and Merry Christmas to you too."

"That was Mrs Cross," she said again. "She just wanted to let us know that the little boy from the school who went missing has made it home for Christmas."

"Oh, what good news," Mr Daley replied.

"And not only that. You remember how his mum was saying Bella would be mauling him, as Dalmatians are bad dogs? Well, Freddie can remember everything that happened. It seems that our little Jingle Bella is another hero. Far from being a danger to him, it was Bella who found the clothes to keep him warm, and also the plastic sheet they were found under. It was her that dragged it over them to protect them from the weather, not him. He even said he could tell she was trying to get him to turn around and go back."

By this time, the Daleys and their dogs had reached their front door. They unlocked it and stepped back into the welcoming warmth of the house. After removing coats, leads and boots, they all crammed together on the sofa to watch the TV.

"I'm not surprised that Bella did all that," Mr Daley said. "She always looks like she's thinking – working things out. She's a clever girl." He warmed his hands on a mug of tea. "Did they find out why the boy was found where he was? No-one had any clue why he would be there. Everyone was looking on his route back home, so where was he going?"

"Mrs Cook said that last year, Freddie had a best friend called Jack, and he often went to his house to play. But then Jack moved away with his family and Freddie hasn't seen him since. It seems he's been struggling to make new friends, and for some reason, that day, he got the idea in his head that he wanted to see if Jack really had gone away or if he was still there. Freddie couldn't remember where Jack lived, but he knew that he'd been able to see and hear trains passing from Jack's house, so that's why he followed the railway track." She paused, then turned slightly teary eyes towards her husband. "He told his mum that Bella is his best friend now, and he's worried she'll get into trouble for coming out of school and following him. His mum has reassured him that she won't, and she's apologised for blaming Bella. I knew she didn't mean it. That was just the worry talking. Mrs Cross is going to tell the local newspapers about it and she says we should get ready for journalists to want to speak to us...again."

"Phew," sighed Mr Daley, puffing out his cheeks. "They really are the Daley's Dog Rescuers, aren't they? We'll have to set up in business." They laughed together at the idea.

Bella was completely unaware of what they had said and what lay in store for her as she'd slept through the whole conversation, but, with a noisy yawn, she woke and slithered off the sofa. Stretching the sleep away, she made her way to the back door, where a pair of keys hung from the lock. Reaching the keys, she stretched up and nosed them, making them jingle like a pair of silver bells.

"Ah, there she is, our Jingle Bella, living up to her name. She wants out and we're being summoned," Mrs Daley chuckled as she got up to let the young dog out into the garden. Lucy and Petra remained asleep on the sofa. Lucy was dreaming about the wasp under the bed upstairs, imagining going up to check on him in the spring and finding him doing loop-the-loops around the spare room, full of vitality after his winter sleep. Petra's paws were twitching. No doubt she was dreaming about chasing something.

"It sounds like we might be about to have another famous dog on our hands," said Mr Daley, when his wife returned from bringing Bella back into the house.

"Oh, it'll be nothing," Mrs Daley waved the idea away. "She'll be in the local papers, but people will soon forget. Next year, everything will go back to normal. There'll be no disappearances, no adventures, and absolutely no rescues. We'll just be normal people with normal dogs."

"Yes dear," Mr Daley agreed. "I'm sure you're right."

The End

Thank You

Firstly, thanks again to the 'secret reader team' who read the pre-publication manuscript for this book. The support from the Daley's Dog Tales Team has been fantastic. Michelle, Daisy, Clair, Ruby, Emma, Rohan, Lindsay and Evie, thank you for your involvement. I'll add my husband Martyn on here too, for his help with proof-reading the final manuscript.

As always, thanks must also go to the fantastic artist, Steve Hutton, who continues to provide such beautiful illustrations and cover art for this series. Likewise, Amanda Horan at Let's Get Booked continues to support me with editorial advice and cover design. This is the eleventh book we've worked on together now, so we're a pretty good team!

To Jayne Hayes, founder of DogLost, thank you for allowing me to mention the organisation in this book. DogLost.co.uk was set up 18 years ago when Jayne's own dog was stolen. It's a volunteer organisation and the biggest dog lost and found community in the UK. They help to reunite stolen, stray and lost dogs with their owners, completely free of charge. Their 150,000 + registered members have helped reunite over 90,000 dogs. After years of campaigning, they, in conjunction with SAMPA (Stolen and Missing Pets Alliance), have finally succeeded in getting a specific crime for 'Pet Abduction' which will give the courts access to hand out the appropriate sentencing to dog thieves, to work as a deterrent against this crime. DogLost runs entirely on donations. If my books can do anything to contribute towards raising awareness of dog theft and puppy farms, I'll be pleased to have played a part.

Finally, we are blessed to have had Bella join our lives. We got her right after losing our beautiful Lucy in 2020 to help us cope with the heartbreak of losing our spotty girl, and she's done just that. Bella has one of the biggest personalities I've ever come across in a dog and she makes us laugh every single day. From jingling keys to ask to be let out, to doing her meerkat impression while receiving tummy tickles, to standing up on her hind legs like a human to get a better look at things, she's a constant source of entertainment. We still miss Lucy Leopard, but we're lucky to have Bella and Petra to cheer us up and provide me with inspiration for stories!

Did you know?

Reading dogs are real. There are a number of charities who are using dogs in schools to raise reading standards of children and also help with their self-confidence and behaviour, as well as their social and emotional welfare too.

The Bark and Read Foundation was set up by The Kennel Club Educational Trust and provides grant aid to charities that send dogs to schools as 'reading volunteers'. These grants help charities and volunteers to provide their services at no cost to schools and enables them to reach more children and young people who can benefit from reading to dogs.

https://www.thekennelclub.org.uk/about-us/charity-work/bark-and-read/

Therapy Dogs Nationwide places temperament assessed dogs with their volunteer handlers into

Primary, Junior, High and SEN schools under their 'Paws & Read Scheme' which is recognised by The Kennel Club.

http://tdn.org.uk/schools-2/

Canine Concern's 'Read to Dogs Programme' is growing all the time as more schools hear about the benefits. Frequently, children find comfort from the dogs and are able to relax when they are with them and the volunteers, which helps them to become more confident readers who are then able to participate more in school work.

https://canineconcern.co.uk/read-to-dogs/

Do you have a reading dog in your school? If so, the author would love to know all about them and the work they do. If you'd like to see your reading dog mentioned on the author's social media, send pictures and information to Helen at:

hhbooks@helenharaldsen.co.uk

Please get permission from the dog's owner and from any humans who appear in pictures too!

About the Author

Helen lives in Cumbria with her husband and a family of horses, dogs, hens, ducks and geese! As well as writing books, she also teaches English and runs a secondary school library.

Visit **www.helenharaldsen.co.uk** to find out more about Helen and to sign up to her mailing list. You'll receive news, updates, opportunities and free, exclusive bonus material linked to HH Books.

Did you enjoy this book? The author would love to see your reviews on Amazon. Please feel free to post your comments and let others know about Daley's Dog Tales and Jingle Bella to the Rescue.

Also By This Author

Daley's Dog Tales:

The Dalmatian that Lost its Spots

Petra and the Dogs in Danger

Amber's Pony Tales:

Little Pearl

The Second Best Pony

Trusting Molly

Amber's Challenge

A Game of Ponies

Stand Alone Books:

A Tale of Two Shoes

For more information visit:

https://www.helenharaldsen.co.uk/

Made in the USA
Monee, IL
20 October 2023